MW00736948

Kite *in a* Hurricane

Kite *in a* Hurricane

SUNIL KAPOOR and SUDHIR KAPOOR

RUPA

Published by
Rupa Publications India Pvt. Ltd 2023
7/16, Ansari Road, Daryaganj
New Delhi 110002

Sales centres:
Prayagraj Bengaluru Chennai
Hyderabad Jaipur Kathmandu
Kolkata Mumbai

P-ISBN: 978-93-5520-769-2
E-ISBN: 978-93-5520-771-5

First impression 2023

10 9 8 7 6 5 4 3 2 1

The moral right of the author has been asserted.

Printed in India

CONTENTS

PREFACE

Every event in life teaches us a thing or two, provided we keep our eyes open, observe things, and contemplate the decisions and actions taken. This book is a collection of these very teachings and, certainly, not a haphazard collection of materials gathered from unlikely sources. We have written these short stories using the best of our experience gained through interactions with friends, relatives, clients, etc., expending time, labour and expense.

The journey of writing stories started with the stupendous success of two of our books—*The Peacock Feather* and *A Ticklish Affair*—thanks to Rupa Publications, which relentlessly marketed them to every nook and corner of the country. The books were declared bestsellers by *Nielsen* and *Hindustan Times*. Many film directors—such as Sujoy Mukherjee of Joy Mukherjee Productions, Abbas–Mustan, Mira Nair, Ravi Chopra, Biswajit Chatterjee, and Charanjit Singh of Northern Lights—waving flags of different banners approached us for stories with quality content. So far, we have succeeded in writing 82 stories on a variety of topics. The stories are based on actual incidents, portraying the realities of life. The same has been envisaged in the following books that have been published:

1. *The Peacock Feather*
2. *A Ticklish Affair*
3. *Punam ka Chand*

4. *Jhoot ke Pair Nahi*
5. *Save the Tiger*
6. *Savere ka Suraj*

One of our closest friends asked us about the source of the ideas that form the basis of these stories. Our reply was to simply keep one's eyes open and observe; to keep one's ear to the ground and listen; and to be curious about the events taking place in one's surroundings. That leads to ideas emerging automatically.

A client of ours once narrated an ordeal of his. He had a bad experience after selling his properties in India and shifting to America to live with his 'American children'. That gave rise to the story 'Invincible America'.

While we were performing yoga on our terrace garden on a windy morning, a kite appeared out of nowhere. This gave us the idea for 'A Kite in a Hurricane'. The story is based on the great success achieved by our father while screening films in Lahore and later by producing films under the banner of M.R. Films Private Limited. The four brothers mentioned in the story are, in fact, our father, Shri Shanker Kapoor, and his brothers—R.I. Kapoor, Radha Krishan Kapoor and Hans Raj Kapoor. The invention in the realm of assisting the visually impaired provided me with the inspiration to pen down 'Yasho Tejaswani'. A court case read in the bar council library of the Delhi High Court became the basis of the story 'Raisina Hills'.

We sincerely hope that readers will find these stories interesting, as all of them are based on true incidents.

ONE

A KITE IN A HURRICANE

In the sultry summer of 1940, the only relief for the perspiring but patient crowd of around a thousand, squatting on the ground of a park near Raja Ram Street (Anarkali Bazaar) in Lahore, was a cool breeze flowing gently from the banks of the river Ravi. The river flowed from the northern part of British India towards the east and formed a canyon as it left the mountains, to wind its way downwards in a serpentine manner into the eastern side of Lahore. The city of Lahore was known as the Paris of British India, with people from all spheres inhabiting it and giving it the colour of the latest fashion and design. People from Lahore—considered middle class—were fun-loving, caring, fashionable and, at the same time, simple and naive. Most of the inhabitants of the northwestern part of British India belonged to the lower middle class and had no source of entertainment.

Quite contrary to the boisterous nature of Punjabi people, the large crowd generated no sound—not even a mumble. This was because people were awed, spellbound, and somewhat perplexed seeing the latest technological invention by the Skladanowsky brothers (Max and Emil) from Germany. The invention, known as Bioscop, had brought a revolutionary change in entertainment in Europe. The four sons of the Sethi household had organized a movie screening at the park, which led to the large gathering that got to witness the Bioscop. At the signal of Ram Sethi, the eldest son, the camera was rolled by an operator with a protruding belly. With that came the astounded looks of the viewers. The camera rolled, screening a silent film, *Raja Harishchandra*, to the mesmerized audience. They could not make out that most of the women playing stellar roles were, in fact, men dressed up as women.

The ecstatic crowd started clapping and cheering as the movie progressed. They loved the screening of the film. Ram Sethi smiled at his younger brother Laxman and whispered, 'Brother, with our determination and the inspiration we got from Dadasaheb Phalke, we have reached where we wanted to reach. See how these people have responded to the Bioscop. We shall soon be screening films in all the colonies of Lahore and then to nearby cities and villages.' Laxman, who was well built and around three inches taller than his elder brother, chuckled. Waving at his younger brother Bharat, he replied, 'Yes, brother, success can be achieved and maintained by a hard worker like you who has managed to stage this show.' Bharat was operating the Bioscop with some difficulty. Though new to the process, he managed to run the film smoothly for a large audience. He spent countless hours studying the intricacies of the projector, learning the proper technique for loading reels into the machine, as well as the usage and function of each part of the massive projector.

While the brothers were celebrating their success, the audience was enjoying every moment of the screening. The film was projected on a loosely bound white sheet attached to the trunks of two trees. Not to be left alone, Shatrughan, the fourth and youngest of them all, said, 'It was great on your part to have bought the film projector for three thousand rupees from the maharaja of a princely state in Punjab. Brother, you may have spent a fortune, but that will go a long way in helping us entertain these people and make a lot of money.'

The Sethi brothers were jubilant as the crowd continued to clap and whistle. The effort put into the film screening was producing an excellent response. The gamble had paid off. Although on 1 September 1939, Adolf Hilter had declared war on Poland and other European countries and had recently bombed cities with a huge disciplined force under his command, it hardly had any effect on the people of Lahore. Hindus, Muslims, Sikhs and Parsis—all had their attention towards the Bioscop. They were there to witness a new form of entertainment. The impact was immense, to say the least.

Soon, the Sethi brothers, who operated the Bioscop, were screening films in Amritsar, which was around thirty kilometres from Lahore. They subsequently covered Jalandhar, Ludhiana, Peshawar, Jamalpur, Rawalpindi, Malerkotla, Quetta and other places in the northwestern provinces of British India. The audience came in large numbers and was enthralled by these remarkable shows that were presented meticulously.

In the year 1940, the charge for each show was one *dhela* for the rows in the front and one *kauri* for the back rows. The phrase 'Yeh samaan kauriyon ke bhaav mila hai (These goods have been purchased for peanuts)' still remains in use.

With the passage of time, the Sethi brothers became one of the pioneers in film exhibition in the northwestern part of British India. They had struck gold in spite of the fact that stalwarts like Prithviraj Kapoor had condemned the Bioscop, proclaiming it had no future. Crowds thronged the parks in which the films were screened. Stage shows were becoming a thing of the past, and the screening of films was emerging as something which appealed to the masses. They could afford the tickets and forget the atrocities of the British for some time at least.

The Sethis went a step further and rented theatres—one of them being Regal Cinema at Mall Road, Lahore. They screened films five times a day, beginning from nine o'clock in the morning. They could not keep track of the money that was coming in on a daily basis and being deposited into their account at the Hindustan Commercial Bank. They soon accumulated enough funds to rope in financiers like Janki Das Kapoor, Sewa Ram Kapoor and young Krishan Kapoor to enter into the arena of film production. The Kapoors were running their business of Hitkari Potteries and Atlas Cycles but agreed to finance the Sethis. The Sethis made sure that the richer they got, the more they helped people in need. This won them the respect of the entire crew, both the on-screen and off-screen staff. The Sethis gained recognition as the foremost philanthropists of Lahore, and their charitable deeds were covered in reputed newspapers such as *Punjab Kesari*.

The success of the Bioscop spread like wildfire and people from other states invited the Sethis to screen their films in their area. When their coffers were filled, the Sethis began the process of producing a film, *Savera*, at Pancholi Studios, located on the outskirts of Lahore. One day, while they were wrapping things up, they saw a boy, around fifteen years old, studying near the panel where the spotlight was fitted. Intrigued, the brothers went ahead and questioned him. The boy told them that he was keen on pursuing his studies, come what may. When they learned about his circumstances, they decided on the spot to fund his education. They arranged for everything and sent the poor boy to a boarding school. Since the shooting was delayed, this incident was a topic of discussion for a few days on set. However, as the shooting progressed, it gradually slipped everyone's mind, including the Sethi brothers, who were accustomed to aiding the underprivileged and disadvantaged members of society.

Savera, which was shot in one year and three months, starred actors like Pran Sikand, Shanker Kapoor, Manorama, Om Prakash and Shyam. Upon its release on 1 January 1944, the Sethis invited and requested famous actor Ashok Kumar and renowned singer Kundan Lal Saigal to inaugurate the premiere of the film. The stars agreed to come all the way from Bombay. Coincidentally, there was a Congress meeting, headed by Jawaharlal Nehru, in Lahore. Around four thousand Congress workers had gathered at the Lahore railway station to welcome Nehru and the others accompanying him. However, the moment the public discovered that Ashok Kumar, K.L. Saigal and Devika Rani were alighting from the same train, they rushed towards the celebrities, leaving Nehru bewildered and amused. Jawaharlal Nehru realized that the film stars were more popular than the leaders of the Congress Party.

Ram Sethi, holding a garland, smiled. He told Laxman, 'Do you realize the power of show business? Ashok Kumar is a bigger crowd-puller than Nehru. The public loves these cine stars and the writing is on the wall. Cinema will surpass all other businesses to come.'

He added, 'Although the production company is MR Films, we shall make movies under the banner of "Shankar Movies".'

While Ram arranged for films to be screened in theatres, Laxman handled the projections. Bharat managed the finances, and Shatrughan handled the crowd and the helpers for their newly formed production company, which had its registered office at house number five, Raja Ram Street, behind Anarkali Bazaar, Lahore. Bharat had the technical expertise to handle the large projection machines used in the show business.

By the middle of 1945, the Second World War had ended. The world was on the path to peace and, as a result, the entertainment industry gathered momentum. On the advice of actor Ashok Kumar, the Sethis shifted lock, stock and barrel to Bombay. They did not realize that this move would have become inevitable two years later due to the partition of India and the creation of West Pakistan and East Pakistan.

In Tinseltown, the Sethis purchased one apartment at the Kamal Mahal building at Marine Drive and another at Colaba. The money that they had transferred from their accounts to the State Bank of India, Colaba branch, was utilized to purchase five theatres—one each in Bombay, Nagpur, Satara, Amravati and Sholapur. Films were showcased not only in these theatres but also in other theatres like Maratha Mandir, Regal and Jubilee, to name a few. The Sethis were making money and growing in status. After India attained independence, their business flourished like never before. They had started throwing lavish parties which were attended by Dev Anand, Sashadhar Mukherjee, Dilip Kumar, Raj Kapoor, Ashok Kumar and others. Later Shammi Kapoor, Joy Mukherjee and Biswajit Chatterjee joined the elite group of film personalities.

While Ram continued to stay at Kamal Mahal, Laxman stayed with his family at Colaba. Bharat and Shatrughan bought houses in the Juhu Vile Parle Development Scheme. Soon, all of them were driving the latest cars, participating in cricket matches with film stars, and even going on picnics to nearby areas with celebrities. The Sethis enjoyed vacations abroad. They lived a dream-like life by achieving success with every film they produced. Joy Mukherjee, Biswajit Chatterjee, Shammi Kapoor and other film stars waited to work for them under the banner of Shanker Movies. The banner was named after the father of the Sethi brothers.

Ram was launching new projects and managing finances from distributors who had mushroomed in big cities like Delhi, Bombay, Calcutta and Madras. He had hired capable writers, and a creative team was constantly at work. Laxman managed the production logistics in close collaboration with the director of the film. Bharat worked as a line producer and technician. He was responsible for breaking down the script and creating line items in a budget plan. He was also supposed to handle human resources. Shatrughan worked as an impact producer, focussing mainly on marketing, distribution of film advertisements, and press and media coverage. He had befriended many journalists, and they gave wide publicity to films produced by the Sethis in their write-ups and articles. The four brothers were still young and brimming with confidence.

In the sixties, portable cameras were invented. This increased the responsibility on the shoulders of Shatrughan. He started organizing outdoor shootings, particularly in scenic places like Kashmir. In 1968, the Sethi brothers announced their magnum opus, *Ashoka: The Great*, along the lines of Hollywood epics like *The Ten Commandments*. The brothers unanimously decided to put all their finance and assets into the making of a big-budget film like *Mughal-e-Azam* or *The Ten Commandments*. But that decision reflected their hubris.

Every movie has its own set of challenges. About two hundred tailors were employed to stitch third-century BC clothing, which was worn during the reign of Ashoka. Megastars were roped in and huge sums were paid to them as signing amounts. Advances were paid to scriptwriters, screenplay writers and dialogue writers. Production assistants were sent to various locations for determining outdoor battle scenes. The production was launched on 15 July 1969. Advances and loans were taken to shoot battle scenes on an open ground near Haldighati in Rajasthan. But certain incidents happened within the span of a month which halted the shooting and plunged the Sethis into debt. It marked the beginning of the closure of one of the biggest production houses of that time.

Ram Sethi, by now around fifty-six years old, received a frightening call from a gangster-turned-extortionist, who asked for fifty lakh as 'protection money'. The figure that they were demanding was beyond the means of the Sethis. They could neither refuse nor pay the protection money demanded by a well-known criminal. Such a demand was something unheard of at that time. The entire budget of the film was one crore rupees and giving away fifty lakh did not make any sense. Nobody had heard of the Bombay Mafia syndicate or about their practice of extortion. Troubles were caused by labour unions but nobody had heard of extortion by the mafia.

Ram received another call from the underworld. He quietly put down the receiver of the black-coloured landline phone and told his family that the caller had threatened to assassinate the brothers one by one if they did not agree to pay the extortion money. There was pin-drop silence in the living room of the family. The brothers now lived together in a huge house at Bandra East. Ram resolved that they would unitedly face the challenge thrown by the gangster. He could not succumb to the demands of this good-for-nothing hooligan. He would not give him the money, come what may. He said to his concerned and worried family, 'I think we should not pay money to this hoodlum who was just a street hooligan some time back.'

Bharat intervened, 'No brother, let's gather fifty lakh from all our distributors and hand over the money. Life is of utmost importance. You know these hooligans have a bloated ego and can take any extreme step.'

Laxman nodded in agreement, while Shatrughan sided with his eldest brother. Shatrughan said, 'Brother, I will talk to my dear friend DGP Manohar Rane and seek police protection from him. Still, we should accumulate some funds, say ten lakh or so, and hand it over to the local mafia.' Everybody agreed to this two-pronged plan.

Three days later, another call came from the same extortionist. The brothers told him that some of the money had been arranged. He asked them to wait till they got another call. On receiving the call, the money was put in a dustbin outside the Mahim church.

Huge advances and loans were taken to pay off the gangster. Half of the extortion amount was paid and a fortnight was sought to arrange the remaining funds. DGP Rane provided security cover for Ram Sethi, stationing Sub-inspector Nimbalkar for his protection.

Ram received another call on 17 January 1970, and the colour drained from his face. The caller said, 'I am speaking on behalf of my boss. Our message for you is to ask Sub-inspector Nimbalkar to resume his duties at the police headquarters and not be your escort. My boss wants you to arrange the remaining twenty-five lakh within a week or take a bullet on your forehead.'

Laxman, who had been silent till then, surprised everyone by opening a bag and taking out a revolver. Placing it on the table, he whispered, 'From now on, I will always be by the side of my elder brother and even use this revolver if the need arises.' Ram looked at him in astonishment and said, 'Are you crazy? From where did you get a licence for a revolver? Who has given you this gun? We are creative people. We cannot even think of using arms. What do you think of yourself, Laxman? Is this some kind of script from a film? This is harsh reality and you must accept it. We must pay these goons and get them off our backs.'

Shatrughan intervened, 'Sorry, brother, I'm the one who arranged for this revolver and gave it to him. DGP Rane has arranged the gun licence for him. I thought it was prudent to take precautions. Sub-inspector Nimbalker remains your escort along with Laxman, who has the revolver in his possession.'

Ram Sethi threw up his hands in desperation. Bharat also spoke up, 'Brother, this is the end of the road. Even if we manage to arrange another twenty-five lakh, we shall be in heavy debt. After this matter gets over, we have to complete the production of *Ashoka*. If we cannot complete the film or if it flops, we shall be hit very badly and our finances would hit rock bottom.'

Ram Sethi assured him, 'Do not worry, Bharat. Once this nightmare is over, we shall complete our film and be back on our feet. All the distributors and exhibitors are going to support us.' The family decided to follow the advice of DGP Rane and seek more time from the hoodlums. Twenty-five lakh rupees was, by no means, a small sum.

While Shatrughan was negotiating with the gangsters and asking for more time, Ram made his usual Tuesday morning visit to the Shri Ram Temple at Versova. He was a pious and religious man. On that fateful day, he went to offer his prayers, along with Laxman, who was always by his side. Unfortunately, Sub-inspector Nimbalkar had fallen ill and could not accompany them. The priest took the garland and other offerings from Ram. He performed the prayers. Ram and Laxman prayed for the much-needed strength to overcome the crisis they found themselves in.

As the brothers came out of the temple, they were confronted by two goons. One of them took out his revolver and fired at Ram while hurling abuses. Ram dodged the bullet, which hit Laxman on his left shoulder. Laxman took out his revolver with his right hand and fired. The bullet missed the two assailants. They, in turn, shot at Laxman and one of the bullets hit him straight in the chest, piercing his heart. His soul left him even before he fell to the ground.

Ram rushed towards a shop that was located around ten yards away from the temple. He hid inside the shop while the shopkeeper and his helper ran out for their own safety. No one wanted to antagonize the assassins. The assailants entered the shop and searched frantically for Ram. Ram was hiding in the bathroom which was behind the shop. The assailants broke open the bathroom door and dragged a frightened Ram Sethi out of the toilet. They pumped seven bullets into him, killing him instantly. The assailants left shouting the name of their boss. They warned: 'Anybody who does not take our don seriously will meet the same fate.'

A few people witnessed the incident, but none of them came out of their hiding places to help the victims. Ram and Laxman lay in a pool of blood until the police arrived and took them to hospital, where they were declared brought dead.

The news spread like wildfire and almost all the newspapers covered it. In the evening at 8.00 p.m., the news was splashed across television. At the mansion of the Sethi brothers, there was utter mayhem. The women of the house and the relatives were wailing uncontrollably. With all the money, power, influence and fame, nothing could save the two brothers. Both the brothers lay on the floor covered under white sheets. They had been riddled with bullets.

Bharat took some anti-depressants and slept for many hours. Shatrughan handled the stream of relatives and friends who kept pouring in. He was in touch with the police and wanted the goons to be apprehended as soon as possible.

Inspector Shinde was assigned the case. He quickly reached the spot where the double murder had taken place. A forensic team collected vital evidence, such as the bullet shells, from the scene of the crime. Two bullets were embedded in a nearby banyan tree, which meant a total of eleven rounds were fired using two revolvers.

Soon, the notorious smuggler and extortionist who called himself Raghu Don was arrested by Shinde. The inspector had been tipped off about the assailants' presence at a restaurant in Borivali. He rushed there with his team and arrested the two assailants after an exchange of fire. Later on, one of them turned approver and spilled the beans. The district court sentenced the shooters to life imprisonment since they had committed the gruesome crime at the behest of their employer. A film producer—a competitor of the Sethis—was found to be a co-conspirator. The extortionist and the co-conspirator were sentenced to seven years of rigorous imprisonment. The news was sensational. It was not a case of extortion but a premeditated murder orchestrated by the Sethis' arch-rival and competitor, BMQ Productions. Shinde worked on this theory since the gangsters would not commit such a crime after receiving half of the extortion money. As time passed, some tranquillity was restored in the Sethi household.

Shatrughan took over the affairs of MR Films Private Limited. The financial situation had gone from bad to worse. Still, he persisted with their magnum opus and set the ball rolling. He was a fighter who refused to give in even when the going was tough. He appealed to the high court against the orders of the district court, seeking stricter punishment for the criminals, languishing in Yerwada Jail. He was hit by an Ambassador while returning from his morning walk at the Juhu beach. The accident was perpetrated by the gangsters. Shatrughan suffered multiple fractures and injuries.

It fell upon Bharat to take up the cudgels on behalf of MR Films Private Limited. He was the one who had to run the show. But he did not have the courage to face the gangsters, creditors and financiers. He could not hold on to the properties owned and mortgaged by the Sethis. He sold the immovable assets one by one, paying off many of the creditors. A sizeable sum was still unpaid. The bungalows at Juhu and Bandra East were sold, and the family shifted to their two-bedroom flat at Colaba. The flat, in fact, was their first purchase after achieving success in the film industry following Partition. Eleven members started living at the Colaba flat in perilous circumstances. They had to sell off their cars and belongings to meet their expenses. Interest had to be paid on loans, and the distributors wanted the film to be completed in order for them to recover their investment. Bharat sold off all the five theatres that the brothers had bought. He had to settle for less than the market price since people had come to know about his financial troubles. Buyers connived to manipulate Bharat into selling the theatres for peanuts. Being weak and timid, Bharat gave in easily.

Even after the theatres were sold, the creditors continued to come for their dues. The loans had been taken at 36 per cent interest, and the amount owed kept growing each day. Many a time, Bharat thought of committing suicide. His wife, Mala, came to his rescue, giving him all her jewellery. On selling the jewellery for a hefty amount, he started gaining confidence. After the assassination of Laxman, his family had shifted to Delhi, where his in-laws lived. The family members living in Colaba barely managed to survive as it was difficult to accommodate so many people in a two-bedroom flat. Bad luck continued to pursue them. Their condition was like that of a kite in a hurricane. Bharat, like a kite buffeted by the winds, was dealing with turmoil. He could neither handle the financial crisis nor manage the household expenses. Shatrughan was indisposed due to multiple fractures, adding to the burden and trauma.

Bharat once grimaced, 'How can God be so cruel to us? We not only have assets to maintain but also kith and kin. Money can come and go but my brothers would never come back to life.' Cars, jewellery and expensive items were a thing of the past. Bharat had taken up a job as a production assistant with a big-banner production house. He had to travel by the local train to the studios.

Mala and Shatrughan were always by Bharat's side. Mala

arranged for some funds from her brother. Bharat was once again coaxed to complete the film that was the dream project of the Sethi brothers. His brother-in-law asked him not to worry about finances and complete the remaining four reels of the film.

The shooting of *Ashoka: The Great* was resumed. The entire team of technicians, along with the actors, was called back. The date of the mahurat was fixed on Ram's birthday. But, on the very first day, a dark cloud descended. Bharat tried to break the sacred coconut. Though he hit it harder than ever, it somehow remained intact. Confused but undeterred, Bharat garlanded the idols of Lord Shiva and Lord Ganesha. To everyone's surprise, blood seemed to be flowing from the eyes of Lord Ganesha's idol. Rumours spread that the gods were unhappy with the producers of the film, which had been jinxed from day one.

Bharat considered these strange occurrences a quirk of fate and postponed the shooting. However, he encountered more problems in his next schedule. When the stars were giving takes and retakes, around a hundred rats entered the studio and ran amok. The female participants got so scared that they left the studio for good. To top it all, an astrologer predicted that the crew would fall seriously ill if Bharat didn't stop shooting. All hell broke loose when some of them had a bout of food poisoning. The unstoppable mishaps left Bharat aghast. Shatrughan called his production in charge and made some inquiries. The investigation revealed that miscreants had put something resembling blood on the eyes of the idol just before the garland ceremony. The coconut which refused to break was brought for inspection. When it was opened, it revealed a thin metal frame specifically designed to keep it from breaking.

Bharat realized that the misfortunes were not just bad luck but a case of sabotage. Further inquiries revealed that the don's hoodlums had purchased some rats from rat catchers and drugged them with sweetmeats. The unconscious rats were put in jute bags. When they regained consciousness, they were released during the shooting of the film to upset the crew. The food poisoning was also the handiwork of the same miscreants, who had purchased and contaminated the food to derail the film. When Bharat reviewed the existing footage, he found that parts of the camera were missing. There were no recordings. These acts of sabotage dashed all hopes of completing the film.

Seeing the state they were in, Mala was very upset. She was the family's pillar of strength. She performed most of the household chores and cooked food for the entire family. She struggled with her weight and could not breathe properly at night. She had to use oxygen cylinders, which added an expense that Bharat could not afford.

It is said that when misfortune strikes, it drags you down into a never-ending spiral of unfortunate events, making you lose all hope. To pull Bharat out of the abyss, Mala decided to take him to a function hosted by her uncle in Ahmedabad. While they were going to attend the function, another mishap occurred. Mala's weight had reached a point where she could not see her own feet, making it difficult for her to get down from the train. Bharat and Mala had decided to get down at the small junction located around ten kilometres before the main station in Ahmedabad. The train stopped there only for a few minutes. Mala's cousins had come to receive them. Her uncle lived nearby. Instead of getting off the train on the platform side, they accidentally stepped out from the opposite side. As no one was there to receive them on the opposite side of the platform, they climbed back onto the train, which had started to leave. Just then, they heard their names being called out by a cousin on the platform side of the station. Bharat leaned out of the train window, waved to his brother-in-law, and shouted, 'We shall get down at Ahmedabad Central Station.' His brother-in-law waved back to confirm as the train gathered speed. For some strange reason, the train screeched to a halt. Seizing the opportunity, Bharat got down again and asked his wife to do the same. As Mala was about to alight from the train, it gave a jerk and started to move. She lost her balance and fell down. Though Bharat raised a hue and cry, the train did not stop. As Bharat watched helplessly, Mala rolled under the wheels. He lost consciousness and fell to the ground. He regained consciousness at the house of Mala's uncle.

After losing two brothers, and with his beloved wife now grievously injured and handicapped for life, Bharat lost all desire to live and gave in to his agony—it was too much for him. He became a recluse, never coming out of his room. He stayed like this for some time. Finally, with the resolve that he would end his life, he left home. After wandering aimlessly for a few hours, he went to the station and boarded a train bound for the north. He reached Delhi. The next morning, he took a bus to Rishikesh near Haridwar, with the sole aim of ending his life in the Ganges, the holy river. As he boarded the bus, he felt that all his lingering worries were gone. The moment he got off the bus, he started puking. Some people were disgusted by the sight, while others expressed pity. Some passers-by didn't even bother to look, while some looked at him with contempt. With the last ounce of his energy, he dragged himself to the river. Looking at the pristine river, he felt certain that this was the end to all his miseries. By drowning his body, he would be released from this world that had only given him pain. For a while now, his life had been like a kite in a hurricane—totally out of control.

He prayed to the Almighty and, remembering his family members, decided to end his life. Before he could jump into the river, a hand grabbed him and pulled him backwards. He was startled as his eyes, swollen from crying, alighted on a blurry, bearded saint. As Bharat wasn't in his senses, he wriggled out of the man's grip and jumped in.

When Bharat opened his eyes, he found himself lying in a bed. He tried to get up quickly, but the moment he did so, he felt his body come apart from the immense pain. He wondered if he was in heaven. As he lay down to rest, he heard a voice. 'Awake already?' Bharat did not respond even after he was called two or three times. He opened his eyes to find the same saint who had attempted to rescue him. The saint smiled at Bharat and left. Bharat was in an ashram, where attendants and nurses took proper care of him.

He mustered up the courage to go out and search for the bearded man. His saviour turned out to be the head of the ashram. On finding out that Bharat was up and about, the saint called Bharat to his room. Despite being sceptical about the saint, Bharat was impressed with his aura and the energy he radiated. Everyone called him Swami ji. The saint politely asked Bharat, 'Son, why were you hell-bent on committing suicide, a thing only weaklings and cowards do?' Bharat took some time and told him about his past. The saint smiled at him and said, 'Do not let your struggles defeat you. Do you see that *sadhvi* serving food? Her name is Rani. She belonged to a rich family settled in Canada. Her husband and three children died in a car accident. She was the only survivor. She has come all the way to Rishikesh to join my ashram. No longer despondent or pessimistic, she has become a light-hearted person who thinks about others. She is now one of us. Her duty is to serve food to everyone at the ashram, and she is quite content with it.'

Seeing Bharat's state, Swami ji added, 'I would suggest that you stay here for some time, though you must not remain idle. First try yoga and meditation, and then join Rani to serve the people. There is so much solace in serving others.'

Bharat could not say no and agreed to live in the ashram for some time. For the rest of his time at the ashram, he was engaged in one thing or the other. He was so tired by the end of the day that the moment he closed his eyes, he fell asleep. After staying there for three months, he realized that he was no longer depressed. He was functioning well and did not entertain any disturbing or pessimistic thoughts about life and his fate. He looked forward to the next day. He was really grateful to Swami ji for the remarkable change in him. From a weak and sulking Bharat, he had turned into a robust and confident Bharat.

He realized that trying to break out of the cycle without understanding one's purpose, just because life may seem unfair, was foolish. He decided that he would continue to serve people for the greater good, both the privileged and the underprivileged, so long as he stayed in the ashram. Swami ji told him that everyone faces some kind of loss that makes life seem unfair and not worth living. But with yoga and meditation, negative thoughts can be converted into positive thoughts. Bharat called up his family and informed them of his well-being.

After working in the ashram for another month, Bharat felt like he was given a new lease of life. He realized that having an attentive ear can ease one's pain. He started writing books based on his encounters and observations. Someone from the media recognized him as the successful film producer of yesteryear. The journalist made use of the opportunity and took his interview, which was published in one of the daily newspapers.

After spending a considerable amount of time at the ashram, Bharat approached Swami ji. He told Swami ji that he would now like to take his leave and embark on a journey to find the means to finish what he and his brothers had started but never completed. As he was leaving the ashram, someone stopped him at the exit gate. The person asked him, 'Are you by any chance Bharat Sethi?'

Bharat was startled and asked him in a shaky voice, 'How do you know me? Who are you, son?' The person replied, 'Sir, please let me remind you that a long time back, you and your brothers helped a fifteen-year-old boy with his education after seeing him study under a spotlight.' Confused, Bharat said uncertainly, 'Did we? Maybe we did ... but I apologize as I do not remember ...'

Then the man, bubbling with confidence, introduced himself as Salil Manchanda. He was the boy the Sethi brothers had helped. He was now the CEO of a company that financed businesses and films. Although Bharat said he was in a hurry, Salil suggested that they catch up since it had been a long time. Unable to refuse, Bharat gave in. They went to the ashram's canteen. While they were having their meal, they started talking about the past. That's when Salil asked, 'Sir, what happened to your dream project? And, what are your brothers doing now?' Salil's question took away Bharat's appetite. There was an awkward pause as Bharat suddenly became quiet. When Salil pressed him, he decided to share the ordeal faced by his family. Upon learning what had happened, Salil was initially baffled. However, he composed himself and calmly suggested, 'I hope I'm not overstepping, but what if I told you that I can help you complete the movie? Would you be willing to take me up on that offer?'

Salil offered to loan money to Bharat and further stated, 'Although you may have been my benefactor and I may be indebted to you, I'm currently in a position to selflessly help you. Along with financing you fully, I would be helping you with the props, equipment, locations, and getting permissions from the authorities. As for the cast and crew, you will be responsible for arranging that.'

Bharat called up Shatrughan and spoke to him. The brothers decided to give their dream project one last shot. After all, they had nothing to lose. Salil pushed the plan and convinced his company's board of directors to have a look at Bharat's proposal. He assured them that they would not regret investing in the film. The finance company approved a certain amount of the loan. Bharat and Shatrughan shot the film with mostly the original cast, but with a new approach and technology. Since Salil and his company were looking after everything, the shoot got completed without any issues.

On the day of the premiere, Bharat's and Shatrughan's families went to the temple at Versova to pray. *Ashoka: The Great* was not only premiered on the big screen, but it was also well received by the audience. The film bagged critical acclaim and went on to become a whopping success. It was dubbed in various languages and became the biggest blockbuster of that year.

Once again distributers made a beeline for the Sethi brothers, and money started pouring in. Shatrughan and Bharat, along with their families, shifted to a better and bigger house.

The Sethi brothers became famous again as all newspapers and magazines covered their success story. They did not forget their past investors and shared the revenue with them. For the Sethis, the days of glory were back again. Bharat and Shatrughan urged Ram's and Laxman's families to come back to Mumbai to celebrate the success of their dream project. *Ashoka: The Great* enjoyed tremendous success, surpassing that of any movie before it.

Shankar Movies became a household name. People flocked to the theatres to watch the movie again and again. The songs and dialogues of *Ashoka: The Great* were on everyone's lips. The movie became a craze in no time.

The kite in a hurricane finally found support and soared high in the blue sky.

TWO

INVINCIBLE AMERICA

Waking up early, Harneet tossed her quilt aside, stepped out of the bed, and dragged herself towards the kitchen, where she found her mother preparing tea. She wished her mother 'good morning' with a hug. Her mother smiled and nodded while putting sugar into the teapot. After arranging the cups, saucers and biscuits on a tray, she asked Harneet to wake up her brother, Bunty. 'It is seven o'clock. Your father will be back from his walk any moment. You know how punctual he is. If he sees someone in bed while we have morning tea, he might throw a fit.'

Karam Kaur, a petite and fair woman, was married to Surjit Singh, fondly referred to as Daar ji. She was the mother of Harneet and Amrik. Both her children were married and settled in the US. Harneet, nicknamed Honey, lived in Long Island, New York, and was married to Dr Amarjit Singh. Amrik—'Bunty' at home—lived in New Jersey with his wife, Kuljit. Both the son and daughter had returned to India after a long time. Karam looked forward to spending quality time with her children.

Seeing her mother alone in the morning, Honey seized the opportunity to raise the topic of her parents shifting to the US. Putting her arms around her mother, she asked her mother to reconsider the decision to not move to the States. To persuade her mother, she started listing the reasons for her aversion to India. Honey stressed that the US had tons of schemes, laws and other beneficial provisions for senior citizens, such as housing, medical facilities, foster system and post-retirement opportunities. In contrast, India had only old-age homes and certain schemes for the elderly. For both the children living far away in the US, their ageing parents' well-being was a cause of concern. Either the parents would have to manage on their own, or stay in private or government old-age homes. If they shifted to the US, they could even join a religious or spiritual organization or some cult. They could happily spend the rest of their days there. To make her point, Honey went to the extent of bad-mouthing India while placing the US on a pedestal.

Being a staunch nationalist, Karam got annoyed. She brushed aside her daughter's claims by stating that she and Daar ji were quite content with their life in India. They had no hesitation in staying at their current residence even if something undesirable were to happen in the future. It was an argument they had had many times before. Moving to the US and leaving everything behind was not something that appealed to the old couple. However, Karam had recently turned sixty. Thoughts of enjoying time with her grandchildren had begun to cross her mind. She cast aside the thought as there was no way her husband would even entertain the idea of leaving India. He was firmly against moving to the US.

Surjit had just retired from a pharmaceutical company. The investments in mutual funds and fixed deposits were churning out a sizeable income for them. With the added pension, they could live comfortably without having to worry about money. Surjit had spent forty years in the company and was well settled in Delhi. Other important reasons for staying in India were his friends and relatives as well as the properties he had—his parents' house besides a spacious house in South Delhi, valued at thirty crore rupees.

Despite her mother's refusal to move to the US even after numerous discussions, Honey went on and on about the nitty-gritty of the American system. Karam expressed her desperation to live with her children and grandchildren, admitting with a tinge of exasperation in her voice that she was lonely without them. Karam started talking about her plight, complaining that there was nobody with whom she could share her thoughts and feelings. Since she had no say in the matter, Karam advised Honey to consult Daar ji about the proposal.

While this discussion was going on, Surjit Singh had entered the house. As he bent down to take off his sneakers, he heard Karam and Harneet arguing. He sat there listening to their argument.

The daughter paused, observing the changes in her mother's opinion about moving to the States. Harneet's husband worked as an orthopaedic surgeon in New York. She had given birth to twins, who were now old enough to be studying in a boarding school close to Nevada. Just when Karam seemed to be giving in, her son burst into the kitchen asking for breakfast. Upon seeing her son, Karam paused and looked at him favourably. Harneet asked her brother to describe his life in the US. Bunty had emigrated to the US after his sister. He got help from his brother-in-law, Amarjit Singh, with both the immigration process and in establishing a business centre at the Twin Towers in Manhattan. Bunty, who was a bit startled, asked his sister not to force their mother if she was not in favour of leaving. He added that their mother was familiar with all the positive and negative aspects of Indian society, and knew how this country functioned. If she still wanted to live here, he was fine with that. He, however, wondered if his mother was okay with being cooped up in India and not exploring the country where her children and grandchildren lived.

No one realized that Daar ji was patiently listening to their conversation. But when he noticed that his children were disparaging their motherland and trying to sway their mother's emotions, he stopped pretending to untie his laces. He raised his voice to ask what was causing all the commotion early in the morning. Seeing Daar ji all of a sudden, everyone froze. Unaware that her father had overheard everything, Honey made Bunty the scapegoat and urged him to continue with what he was saying. Now, it was Bunty's turn to wax lyrical about the miracles of the US. From huge lawns to private swimming pools, malls to theatres, bikes to cars—everything was described in such an exaggerated manner that it seemed like having lawns and pools was pretty normal for a regular upper-middle-class family in the US. He went on to add that within a span of ten years, he had made a fortune and was now living in a villa in a rather posh neighbourhood. Bunty's glowing description of life in the US stressed the fact that everyone was happy in that wonderful country.

Both the parents were listening to their children. While Daar ji remained indifferent, Karam paid attention to the positive aspects of the US. She was now willing to heed their entreaties. Though Karam showed signs of weakening, Bunty and Honey observed that she chose to remain silent. It didn't take Bunty and Honey much time to figure out the reason for her silence. Having grown up in a strict environment, where their father's decisions had to be agreed upon, they could understand the pressure and loneliness Karam felt. Bunty decided to play the sympathy card and urge his father to let his mother stay with her children and grandchildren.

Surjit Singh was a man who led a disciplined life. He had strong views and a mind of his own. He seldom agreed with others and was resistant to their proposals. He only listened to his close friend Roshan. Before Bunty could start again, he said,

'Dear children, let me tell you what Roshan told us in the park.' He then shared with them an entire lecture on the mistakes made by senior citizens after they cross sixty, and the ways in which these can be avoided.

'First of all, one should be content with what one has—that is, one should count one's blessings and not one's troubles. Second, one should take care of one's health and go for regular medical check-ups to avoid falling ill and paying hefty hospital bills. One should also have a health insurance plan. Third, one should not use credit cards blindly. People splurge and forget to pay the credit card bills on time. They have to then pay an exorbitant amount as interest. Most credit-card holders are not even aware of the high rate of interest. Fourth, one should not overspend on parties, clubs and holidays—thinking there is no tomorrow. Fifth, one should give one's property and savings to one's children only through a will and not any time before death, unless it is absolutely necessary.' He concluded the sermon.

Bunty intervened, 'Daar ji, we don't need any money. You used your entire provident fund to send me to the US. We don't want a penny from you. We are extremely rich. The US has been kind to us.' He added that the mistakes Roshan Uncle pointed out were mistakes made by Indians and not Americans. Surjit, now disapproving of Bunty's self-absorption, shrugged and commented, 'It's not just Indians. I am sure the senior citizens in the States also make similar mistakes. And dear son, it is not the US that has been kind to you, but Waheguru.'

'No, Daar ji,' Bunty replied. 'In my country, senior citizens are very smart. They start living their lives only after retirement. They don't let sentiments and emotions cloud their judgement. According to their philosophy, we have one life and every person has the right to enjoy it. This is different from Indian culture, where everything revolves around family and children.'

For the first time, Surjit paused. He was taken aback by what his son had just said. 'Bunty, isn't that a wrong paradigm? And what exactly do you mean by "my country"? You may be living in America but your roots are here in India.' In response, Bunty argued that the place where he and his family resided was now his country—and that he loved it. He was about to continue but seeing his father's disappointment, he quickly changed the subject. Surjit was not someone who could be swayed easily so he decided to stay quiet. This made the atmosphere awkward. Harneet took the reins of conversation from her brother and expressed her admiration for Roshan Uncle's insights. 'Well, Daar ji, these are very good suggestions. But please don't let them deter you from shifting to the US. Consider our request seriously. Do whatever you want with your properties. We are not concerned about that. Just remember that time is passing. We want all of us to be together, stay together, and enjoy life together.'

Even after such a lengthy argument, both the parents remained silent. That's when Bunty lost his cool and raised his voice disrespectfully. Bunty told his father that India, which Daar ji was very attached to, had not given him much. Even after giving forty years of his life, all Daar ji got in return was forty-five lakh at the time of his retirement, whereas Bunty earned the same amount in four months and his brother-in-law in just a month in the States. Bunty also mentioned that Daar ji was lucky to have got a plot of 4,500 square feet at a pocket-friendly rate thirty years ago, thanks to his membership of the North Indian Punjabi Colony. Otherwise, with just forty-five lakh rupees, he would not have been able to get such a luxurious place in the present time.

Hearing Bunty talk like that, Honey stepped in and told her brother not to be disrespectful to their father. She went on to say, 'If they do not wish to shift to the States, let them be here. We would keep coming to Delhi to look after them.' Bunty looked at his sister in surprise. She was the one who had raised the issue, and now she seemed to be doing an about-turn.

Surjit turned to his daughter and gave her a pat on the shoulder. Then, taking a deep breath, he informed his children and his wife that after discussing the matter with Roshan, he had decided to sell his properties in India and shift to the US. He also mentioned that he would share a portion of the proceeds with his children. Bunty and Honey looked at him in amazement. This was the first time their father had shown any flexibility in his adamant stance on staying in India.

'Oh, Daar ji,' said Karam, 'I am so happy that I don't have words to express my joy.' Seeing Karam happy, Surjit was proud of his decision. Bunty, convinced that his persuasion had finally taken effect, told Daar ji that he would now leave to freshen up, after which he would call Kuljit, aka Kuki, to relay this news. He said, 'She will be delighted to have you there, and to get a chance to explore the US with you two. The kids will also be overjoyed to have their grandparents with them.'

After her brother left, Harneet said, 'We will apply for your immigration visa and will soon shift you lock, stock and barrel to New York. We siblings will share the cost of your tickets. One day, you will thank us for persuading you to move to the US. India is no longer a safe place to live in, especially for elderly people.'

Turn by turn, till long after breakfast was over, Honey and Bunty rambled on about the wonders of America and the ills of India. They were thrilled that Daar ji was finally willing to make the move that they had been pitching for a long time.

That same evening, an event took place that made Daar ji glad that he had decided to shift to the States. On the evening of 22 December 2000, a major terror attack took place at the Red Fort in New Delhi. It was carried out by Bilal Ahmed Kawa, the leader of Lashkar-e-Taiba. Several soldiers and three civilians were killed. Ashok Kumar, the son of a close friend of Daar ji's, was critically injured in the attack. The media described the attack as an attempt to derail the India–Pakistan peace talks. The Red Fort attack shook the entire country. Surjit was visibly shaken after hearing the news. He rushed to Ram Manohar Lohia Hospital, where his friend received him with tears in his eyes. Ashok Kumar was battling for his life, and there was little hope of survival. A few hours later, he succumbed to his injuries.

The next day at Ashok's funeral, Surjit vowed to try his best to settle down in America, not come back to India, and keep his family safe. That night when the house was mourning the death of the young boy, Bunty, who seemed detached from the grief, couldn't keep the news of Daar ji's decision to himself and called up his wife, Kuljit. Before he could even exchange pleasantries, the anxious wife asked, 'Tell me, are they selling their properties or not?' Bunty hesitantly replied, 'Yes, and Daar ji has hinted that he will share a significant portion of the sale proceeds with us.' Kuljit was thrilled; she couldn't believe her ears. 'Great, then let them come here. You have given me the best news. Their properties are worth a fortune. With the money, we will be able to buy four properties in the States. Nobody I know has millions of dollars; most are broke and can hardly pay their EMI. All our loans will get squared up. We will not need to take any educational loans for our children. God, I can't wait to lay my hands on so much money. We'll be rich. I can't wait to tell Dr Amarjit about this fantastic development.'

She hung up. Bunty was dumbfounded. She did not even inquire about his well-being, her only interest being in the sale proceeds. Soon, Honey and Bunty left for America, bidding farewell to their parents. They were all smiles as they had accomplished their mission.

Once the decision was made, things moved quickly. Within three months, the properties were sold. They fetched thirty-seven crore rupees. Surjit and his wife decided to gift half the sale earnings to their two children and keep the other half for their use and expenses. Surjit also encashed all his investments, which amounted to another sixty lakh rupees. He sent remittances of nine crore each to his children. He now had a capital of sixteen crore and sixty lakh rupees, sufficient for him and his wife to spend the rest of their lives comfortably in the States, enjoying their time with their children and grandchildren. He had also paid the capital gains tax on the sale of the property.

Before leaving, Surjit threw a lavish party for all his relatives and friends. The next morning, they handed over the keys of the house they had lived in for thirty years to the builder who had bought the property. They left for the airport to take a flight to their new life in 'Invincible America'. Daar ji got a little emotional while bidding goodbye to his close friends and handing over the keys of his house. Karam Kaur, however, was all smiles.

As he leaned back in his seat in the first-class cabin of Air India, Surjit reflected on his decision and smiled quietly to himself. Bunty had indeed been right. He turned to his wife and whispered in her ear, 'America, here we come!' Karam, meanwhile, was happily lost in her own reverie. She imagined the joy she would get from giving her grandchildren some quality time—no longer limited to rushed visits that always seemed too short. She said, 'You know, Daar ji, I will finally be able to attend to each child personally. I will make so many delicious Indian dishes that they'll forget about American food.' Daar ji nodded in affirmation, and they went on discussing the possibilities of their new life as the plane began its descent to New York. From the window, they could see the Statue of Liberty. They were finally in America—the 'Invincible America'.

Soon, the pilot announced that all passengers should fasten their seatbelts as they were about to land. Surjit looked out of the window and saw the plane circling the Statue of Liberty and the Twin Towers before it finally landed at the JFK Airport in New York. The entire family was at the airport to welcome them. Their four grandchildren—Bunty's son and daughter as well as Honey's twins—had grown taller since they had last met. The grandchildren felt a bit awkward and reluctant to embrace their grandparents in public. Nevertheless, the grandparents were here now, and, gradually, Karam would help her American grandchildren imbibe Indian values. Karam was pleasantly surprised to see her daughter-in-law, Kuljit, who was all smiles on their way from the airport to their house in New Jersey.

As they settled into Bunty and Kuki's house, a feeling of contentment washed over Karam. All that mattered was that the entire family was around them now. Karam didn't mind a bit when everybody set off early in the morning for work and school. Kuki had a job in the United Nations office as a record-keeper. Bunty had his office in one of the Twin Towers. Both grandchildren went to school after bidding goodbye to their grandparents. Everyone seemed to be in a hurry, but the grandparents were happy. They had to acclimatize themselves to this new environment.

Surjit got in touch with his cousins in New York, but they too didn't seem to have much time for him. They seemed to be rushing to their workplaces whenever he called them. Everyone seemed to be in a hurry in New York. Surjit and Karam were surprised that even the grandchildren were so occupied in their daily chores that they hardly had any time for their grandparents. Bunty and Kuki could only be present with them wholeheartedly on weekends, when they did not go to work.

Karam had taken full control of the kitchen, and Kuljit was happy about it. Kuljit despised cooking. Although several months had passed, Surjit and Karam still struggled to settle down in the US. With various things cropping up, Karam was pushed to the edge. Surjit could understand his wife's disappointment and tried to console her. He said, 'Karam, these Americans are very hardworking people. To survive, they have to be disciplined and get to work or school on time. Otherwise, there could be trouble with their bosses. They have to do everything themselves. There are no helpers available here. People prefer to send their kids to day care as hiring maids and nannies can be very expensive. Household chores—everything from laundry to ironing—are done only once a week.'

After considering this for a moment, Karam said, 'No, Daar ji, all is not well. I've seen defiance in the eyes of Kuljit. She doesn't seem to value our stay in her house. When they stayed with us in Delhi, the house belonged to everyone. Here it seems that we are living in *her* house, that it's not our house at all. She has often thrown hints that I should not touch things in the kitchen. Once she even said, "Please stick to your room. You have no idea how to operate American appliances. This is not India." This is what she said to me, Daar ji.' Karam was visibly upset. 'And, she's trying to create distance between me and the grandchildren by talking like this in front of them. There is indeed a change in her. She is not the same old Kuljit that used to agree with me while she lived in our house, before Bunty left for the States. She never spoke in the manner in which she does now. I think we have made a mistake by coming here.'

Surjit tried to reassure her. 'Karam, what is said is not as important as how it is said. What is said only reaches the mind, but how it is said reaches the heart. And there is no way to win the minds of Kuki and her children without winning their hearts. That's what we should focus on.'

He continued, 'Karam, be positive and give yourself some

time. Relationships get better as time passes. All will be well. We should adapt to their lifestyle and not expect them to adopt the way we were living in Delhi. Karam, be like a river, a crystal-clear river, flowing happily. When there are obstacles in the way, a river finds a new way to flow. So, when there are obstacles here in America, find your way around them and keep flowing.'

'Daar ji, that's easier said than done,' Karam replied, her voice tinged with regret. 'I have already started to lament the fact that we sold our lovely, spacious home and came here. We were not rich, but we were living a good life. Now I have to bear one insult after another.'

'Don't regret, my dear Karam. I am planning to start a business soon—a convenience store, a drug store, or something like that. We will both sit at the counter and run the store. That way, you will not have to deal with Kuljit. We will also get to spend time together and explore this beautiful city.' However, Karam could not be consoled. 'What is beautiful about this city, Daar ji? We've already seen it. Manhattan has only buildings and buildings, nothing else. The Empire State Building, the Twin Towers, Crisil Tower—they all look the same to me. No Daar ji, you will agree with me one day. We have committed a blunder by selling our properties and giving a significant amount to these Americans. In a new country, we are dependent on them—even for our daily needs.'

Surjit persisted, 'No, Karam, you are wrong, and one day I will prove it to you. True, Harneet and Bunty may be in awe of the US, but they do love us. Blood is thicker than water. They were born and brought up in India, and they will never be disrespectful to us. I can't be certain about that when it comes to Kuljit since she is our daughter-in-law. She may not treat us with respect. But it is different with Bunty and Honey; I can guarantee their love for us. After all, Indian values run in their blood.'

'But, Daar ji, you must have realized it in your heart, even though you will not admit it, that things are not the same. I can feel distance and tension growing between us and our children.'

Despite her worries, Karam felt calmer. Surjit was always the wise one. His words had presented things in a different light. Perhaps, Kuki was not deliberately treating her badly. Like everyone else, she could be in a hurry to get things done and reach her workplace on time.

As the days passed, Karam and Surjit tried their best to adjust to their new lifestyle in the States, living with strangers who once used to be their children. Time passed and Karam Kaur somehow accepted the treatment meted out to her by her daughter-in-law.

On the morning of September 11, Bunty was running a bit late as he headed to his office. It started as an ordinary day, but at 8.46 a.m. while walking towards the the Twin Towers to enter the building where his office was situated, he saw a plane crashing into the upper floors. The sound of the impact was deafening. 'Oh my God … Oh my God, what's happening?' Bunty screamed. He had been delayed for work due to an argument with his mother about his wife's disrespectful behaviour, which had gone from bad to worse. As it turned out, the argument delayed his departure for the office and ultimately saved his life.

By that time, hundreds of people had gathered at a safe distance and were looking up in shock at the top floor of the west tower which was on fire. A plane had flown directly into the Twin Towers, and no one could believe what they were seeing. 'What a terrible accident,' said a bystander. Bunty was crossing the Millennium Hotel, located directly across the road from the Twin Towers on Church Street. In a short while, a second plane flew directly into the other tower in front of his eyes. The tower went up in flames. As the second plane collided, the explosion was much bigger. Debris, dust and smoke filled the surroundings. People were running in all directions, trying to save themselves.

Bunty watched in horror as the enormity of the disaster hit home. He had no idea what to do next. Should he rush to his office and retrieve some critical documents and the money kept in his safe? Or, should he run from the site in case something else happened? In his gut, he realized that this was no accident. It was an attack on America, on what he had always thought of as 'Invincible America'. He was in a daze. He could see people trapped on the top floors. Engulfed in an inferno, they were throwing tables and chairs to break windows in a desperate attempt to escape. Others were hanging out of windows, screaming for help. To Bunty's horror, he saw two men fall from the tower and meet their death.

Bunty's instinct told him to get as far away from the towers as possible, so he began running towards Battery Park. He could hardly believe that just two days ago, on September 9, he had taken his parents to see the Statue of Liberty and they had caught the ferry from Battery Park. Now everything was in complete chaos. 'Waheguru,' Bunty muttered, 'what is happening? There are thousands of people trapped in the two buildings.' The towers once showcased American power and achievement. Now they were crumbling in front of his eyes. First one, then the other, collapsing and sending debris flying everywhere. Manhattan was soon covered in a cloud of smoke and dust, with bits and pieces of wreckage strewn about. The heat emanating from the fire was intense. Like him, others were running away, covering their face and eyes to protect themselves from the thick cloud of smoke and dust that had engulfed the area. Pandemonium reigned, and even the police officers were powerless to control the chaos. America's most powerful city had been hit, and nobody knew what to do.

It was a brutal blow to the nation's ego, shattering the illusion of invincibility.

Bunty felt like he was in a daze. The 1,362-foot building, once the tallest in the world, lay in ruins. America, the most powerful nation in the world, had been brazenly attacked by terrorists. He instinctively knew that the world would not be the same again after this. America would not take this lying down. It would avenge this audacity and wouldn't let this heinous attack go unpunished.

As he reached the river, a police boat arrived. He jumped into it, desperate to get to safety. As the boat began to move, he looked back at what was left of the Twin Towers. Everything was in a shambles. The attack had ruptured America's power and influence, and the country would never be viewed as invincible again. The sight was overwhelming, with debris falling like ticker tape, stricken birds flying aimlessly, and columns of smoke swirling over the entire block. The heat and dust had left Bunty's mouth dry. Next to him, an American, clutching his briefcase, blood streaming down his face, cried out in anguish, 'My son is in there. My son is in there. I have a feeling that he has died.'

As the boat moved away to the other side, Bunty observed others sitting beside him, their shoulders hunched, their faces white and stricken. Upon docking, the police provided him with first aid and told him to wait for an hour at a nearby makeshift sanatorium. The city's subway system had been shut down, as were the highways leading into it. All train and bus services had been suspended. All government offices, along with the United Nations building, had been evacuated. The eerie silence was pierced only by the scream of sirens and the shouts of firemen and paramedics, as they worked tirelessly to navigate the ocean of dust and waste that now filled the air from the thick smoke-filled rubble, which had once stood as the Twin Towers.

Television reports later revealed that the September 11 attacks were a series of four coordinated terror attacks by the Islamic extremist group, Al-Qaeda. In those attacks, almost three thousand people lost their lives, six thousand or more were injured, and infrastructure and property worth at least ten billion dollars were damaged. The terrorists were led by Osama Bin Laden. President Bush was attending a school function during the incident. Andy Card and Condoleezza Rice were provided with delayed information that a plane had crashed into the North Tower. Card's response was, 'Oh, that would be a terrible accident. Maybe the pilot suffered a heart attack or something.' However, when he was informed about the second plane crashing into the other tower, he immediately realized that it was a deliberate attack on America.

It took Bunty six hours to reach home, where he found his parents and other family members terrified and praying for his safety. The family spent the entire day in front of the television as reporters pieced together what had happened on the morning of September 11. The terrorists, nineteen Al-Qaeda members, hijacked four passenger flights operated by two US carriers, leaving from airports in the northeastern US and bound for California. American Airlines Flight 11 crashed into the North Tower of the World Trade Center, followed by United Airlines Flight 175 smashing into the South Tower just minutes later. The third flight crashed into the Pentagon, the headquarters of the US Department of Defense. The fourth flight, heading towards Washington, D.C., was prevented from advancing by courageous passengers. It crashed into a field in Pennsylvania. Together, these events constituted the deadliest terrorist attack in human history.

The destruction of the World Trade Center and the surrounding infrastructure had a devastating impact on the economy of lower Manhattan, and its effect rippled across the global market. Bunty, too, was impacted by the attack. He had considered the US invincible until now. This belief was shattered when his plush 27th-floor office, along with all his investments in furniture and fixtures, crumbled to the ground in front of his eyes. Everything was gone. Gone too was his main source of income which came from the other offices housed in the Twin Towers. His entire business collapsed in a single move made by Al-Qaeda. He was so devastated, and his faith so shaken, that he even contemplated suicide at one point. Bunty had made a down payment for his pending EMIs towards his office, which had been destroyed in one stroke. He could not control his anger. 'Al-Qaeda ... I feel like killing these Islamist terrorists with my bare hands. They have brought so much trouble. I just can't explain it to you, Daar ji.'

His father, trying to console him, patted his shoulders and said, 'Son, be honest when in trouble, and be silent when in anger—things will work out for the better. That is what life management is all about.' A tearful Bunty moaned, 'Daar ji, I am left with no money. Just a few days after that wretched bin Laden struck, I lost everything.'

After seeing his son's precarious situation, Surjit gave him most of his savings to help him rebuild his life. This pleased Kuki but irked his son-in-law, Dr. Amarjit. Despite earning well, he wanted his father-in-law to be fair to both the children. Realizing this discrepancy, Surjit gave some of his savings to Dr Amarjit as well. Almost the entire amount that Surjit and Karam had received from the sale of their properties had been distributed between their two children. They were penniless within months of arriving in America. Bunty tried setting up his business again, but the economy was shaky and he ended up losing a lot of money. Other investments that he had in shares and securities were also lost due to the steep downward fall that occurred when Wall Street, which had been closed due to the attack, reopened. Within a few days, America witnessed the worst market crash since 1935. And for Bunty, all was lost after the September 11 attack.

Surjit was shocked when he learned that Bunty had not insured his premises in the Twin Towers. It was a total loss. Another bitter truth surfaced as he slowly learned that his children were maintaining their lavish lifestyle through bank loans, and heavy EMIs had to be paid every month. So, a large amount was to be paid for the mortgage on their houses and offices. There was hardly any money in their bank accounts. All this came as a rude shock to him.

As the troubles increased, so did the quarrels between Kuki and Karam. Bunty tried to sort things out between his mother and wife but failed miserably. One constant source of tension was a minor issue. Karam made Indian cuisine, which neither Kuki nor her kids liked. They were used to a different lifestyle and different food habits. They preferred American food and were more comfortable with packaged food. This Indian grandmother could not understand how they could prefer such food over the fresh meals that she toiled over every day. Nor could she understand the 'it's my life, and I will live the way I want to' attitude of theirs. It also deeply distressed Karam that the children did not visit the gurdwara at all and had not been there even once since she had arrived in the US. She had not seen even her children visiting the gurdwara in the two years she had been in New York.

As the arguments in the house escalated, Bunty had no option but to give his parents some space. The old parents reluctantly agreed to Bunty's request to shift to Honey's house at Long Island for a month or so. Once they shifted, Surjit and Karam found, to their dismay, that Bunty and Kuki had simply forgotten about them. They did not even call them. Reassuringly though, Honey, unlike Kuljit, took it upon herself to make her parents comfortable. They had barely settled down in their daughter's home when

Surjit received a call from Roshan. Roshan requested that Surjit help his son, who would soon be arriving from India to start a job in New York.

Without hesitation, Surjit told Roshan that his son was most welcome to stay with them at Long Island till he found accommodation of his own. Surjit's gesture of hospitality was not appreciated by Amarjit, who curtly told his father-in-law that his home was not a guest house where anybody could walk in and stay. Amarjit retorted, 'Dad, we are not used to people staying with us. Even your staying here is a bit of an intrusion, but we cannot help it. However, we can't just allow anyone to barge in and stay in this house.'

When Honey tried to reason with her husband, he became furious and threw a cup of hot coffee at her. 'Your parents have not been fair to us,' he shouted at the top of his lungs. 'They have given all their savings to Bunty after the September 11 attack and absolutely nothing to us.' The hostility was palpable and Amarjit's barbs only increased every day. In order not to create further disharmony in their daughter's family, Surjit and Karam decided to leave their home. They had also by now realized that neither their son nor their son-in-law was earning millions as told to them in Delhi. They just lived off EMIs.

Surjit could not handle the insults from his son-in-law anymore. He decided he would start his own small business. They also decided that they would now live independently. When they told their children that they were taking a small one-bedroom apartment in Flushing, to their surprise, neither Bunty nor Honey stopped them. They seemed almost relieved at getting their parents out of their respective houses. Things had drastically changed in the past two years. His children had changed colours like a chameleon, after having received a large chunk of money from him.

Heartbroken at the lack of concern from their children, the

parents shifted their belongings to the tiny apartment at Flushing and tried to survive on the meagre amount left with them. Surjit somehow managed to cobble together enough money to purchase a 7/11 drug store. He first looked at a store on 36th Street in Manhattan but then, persuaded by the broker, bought a 7/11 in the Bronx.

One evening, after closing his 7/11 drug store, Surjit was walking towards the Bronx subway station to catch the 9.20 train to Flushing. It was dark and he was alone when a mugger stopped him with a knife and demanded his wallet. Despite being sixty-four years old, Surjit was a fearless Sikh who always carried a kirpan with him. Not the one to get scared easily, he grabbed the mugger by his shirt, swung him to the ground, and gave him a thorough beating. The mugger shouted for help, and two of his accomplices arrived. One hit Surjit with a club while the other attacked him with a nearby trash can. The three muggers ruthlessly beat Surjit until a police car arrived, causing them to flee.

Surjit's life was saved by a hair's breadth. He was nevertheless grievously injured in the attempted robbery and rushed to Bronx Hospital by the police. After taking down Surjit's number, the doctor called his wife. Hearing about Surjit's condition, a panicky Karam called Bunty for help. However, Bunty was in a late meeting and did not answer despite several calls from Karam. Karam then called Kuljit, who promised to tell Bunty what had happened but conveniently forgot to do so.

Karam dropped the idea of calling her daughter, fearing a backlash from her husband. Instead, she approached a neighbour who drove her to the hospital. She was told that Surjit was out of danger but would need to spend at least two weeks in the hospital. None of her children came to visit, and Surjit signalled to his wife to not call them at all. He had by now realized that his children had made a devious plan to coax him into selling his properties so that they could get the proceeds. Surjit was discharged from the hospital after a few days but had to pay a hefty sum since he had not managed to buy medical or accident insurance due to a paucity of funds.

When Surjit returned to work, he was informed that he had been duped by the broker who sold him the place for his 7/11 store. Surjit had wanted to understand the business and the daily sales figures before investing his last bit of savings. The store's owner suggested that Surjit spend a week in the store, and then take a call. He could observe the way the store was handled and decide if the sales were up to the mark or not. Surjit did not understand that he was being set up. The owner had hired a bunch of unemployed African American boys and paid them to frequently buy items from the store. At night, they would return the same items to the owner. Completely unaware of the game that was being played, Surjit was left with the impression that the store attracted plenty of customers and that the business was thriving. He decided that it would be a good investment and handed over the last of his savings to buy the store. It was only a few weeks later, seeing so few customers enter the store, that Surjit realized that something was amiss. He found and accosted one of the boys he had earlier seen regularly coming into the store and buying several items. That was when he found out that the broker and the store's owner had hired a bunch of locals to pretend to be fake customers for a week. The plan was to lure Surjit into buying the store, which was incurring losses. Disheartened, Surjit told his son and daughter how he had been tricked. They, however, blamed him for being gullible and foolish. They said that he should have known better. Angry at the scammers, Surjit lodged a case against the broker and the store's owner. There was, however, no hard evidence to prove the fraud. No headway could be made in the case.

And then one day, Surjit made a decision. 'Enough of this paradise called America,' Surjit said bitterly to his wife. 'Let's go back to Delhi. I miss my morning walks, and I miss my friends and relatives. What a blunder we have committed by selling our properties and coming to this wretched place. No one has time for us. Our children and grandchildren took what they could from us and then just abandoned us. As long as we had money, they were ready to touch our feet. Now they don't even take our calls, let alone visit us here in Flushing. We've spent the worst time of our lives in America. The last four years have been like a slow death sentence. This place is as full of scammers and hideous people as a colander is full of holes.'

Karam did not fully understand the phrase, but she could see her husband's agony and his desire to be back in Delhi with his friends. Surjit had run into huge losses at the store and had no option left but to file for bankruptcy and liquidation. It was an admission that the business had failed and he had no money to pay his debts—the only remedy left to avoid imprisonment. He closed the store and eventually booked tickets for New Delhi on Kuwait Airways. The flight took a much longer route to reach Delhi, but it was the cheapest and only one they could afford. Neither of their children came to see them off at JFK Airport when they departed. Karam kept looking around for her children before entering the security screening, but no one showed up. She spent the long journey of several hours weeping and feeling deeply depressed. How could something, which was to be a paradise of family togetherness in a dream nation, turn into such a nightmare? Surjit tried to console her but the tears wouldn't stop.

After a long flight, including a long wait in transit, they finally landed in Delhi in the middle of the night on 12 March 2005. Four of their relatives had come to receive them in two cars and that gave them some solace. At least people in India were not like the people they encountered in the US, and it was nice to see that nothing much had changed in Delhi in the last four years. It was such a relief to be held in the warm embrace of relatives with whom they could share their pain.

For three months, they stayed at Karam's nephew's house before shifting to a one-bedroom apartment in Amar Colony. Gone were the days when they had lived in a bungalow of 4,500 square feet in New Friends Colony, with a battery of maids in attendance. Now, everything had to be done by Karam, who could barely walk due to acute arthritis. She had been diagnosed with pneumatic arthritis that was gradually morphing into Parkinson's disease. The stress of the experiences in the States seemed to have taken a toll on her health. Her relatives would visit often, especially her nephew Jasdeep. The nephew also helped his uncle find a job as a salesman in a shop selling sarees and suits in Karol Bagh.

Surjit struggled to do justice to the job because of his ailing wife who needed him frequently. Karam yearned to see the faces of her two children and was heartbroken by all that had happened in the US. In contrast to their experiences in the States, friends and relatives here continued to meet them. They even offered financial assistance to Surjit, who politely declined due to his self-respect. Their financial situation was perilous, and things were about to become worse. Karam suffered a brain stroke. She had to be given a specific injection within three hours of the stroke. She lay in the government hospital's general ward while her husband ran from pillar to post trying to find the money for the injection. Jasdeep came to their rescue and managed to arrange for the required injection. Karam was saved in the nick of time.

What a mistake it was to have moved to the US, Surjit kept thinking. What a blunder! Their wonderful life was destroyed by one wrong decision. They should not have been so gullible to believe their children's promises of paradise and more time together. It was all a farce, and now it was too late. After two months in the hospital, Karam was finally discharged and she came back home in a wheelchair. Her husband, who was now sixty-six years old, was also seeing his health deteriorate. He was suffering from bronchial asthma due to Delhi's pollution, and stress and old age had also caught up with him. Both were in a pitiable condition. There was neither a phone call nor any message from their kids in the US. The parents had nothing left to give their children and were only seen as a liability. Despite this, Surjit was not going to live his life as a victim.

Once he recovered, he approached Roshan to help him set up a business. Roshan suggested that he start by packing some of his products for a fee. Within a few days, Surjit launched his own little business packing Glucose D for Roshan, who had a manufacturing unit in Okhla Industrial Estate. Surjit worked tirelessly. He had spent forty years in a pharmaceutical company and now all that experience came in handy. His business grew; he soon established a decent-sized small-scale industrial unit in Sant Nagar, next to East of Kailash. In the next seven years, the business grew further and Surjit was able to rent a larger factory in Sector 11 in Noida under the name of Medsystems Inc. Here he manufactured paracetamol, hydroxychloroquine tablets, sanitizers, among other things. Years passed and from the small one-room apartment, the couple shifted to a decent three-bedroom flat at the D Block of North Indian Punjabi Society at New Friends Colony.

In 2019, as he celebrated his 79th birthday, his business crossed a turnover of two crore rupees. He enjoyed the credibility he had in the pharma industry and his products had established a market of their own. Karam recovered from her brain stroke, and Surjit kept a maid to help her out. In December 2019, a novel strain of coronavirus began to surface in Wuhan, China. Within a few weeks, it spread to hundreds of countries around the globe infecting people everywhere. On 11 March, the World Health Organization declared it a pandemic—Covid-19, as it came to be called. Medical research revealed that once infected, Covid-19 caused respiratory tract infections and could be fatal. The only way to avoid being infected was to raise immunity levels and sanitize oneself and wear a face mask. Surjit had already established a unit in the Okhla factory which excelled in making N-95 face masks.

Surjit had no trouble getting his overdraft limits enhanced by his bankers, who also saw this for the incredible business opportunity that it was. Sanitizers, paracetamol and face masks were being demanded by almost every shopkeeper and chemist. The old man worked day and night servicing orders. Demand kept increasing, and he quickly set up a new factory in Greater Noida with a staff of over hundred people. He soon became the lead manufacturer for the three items. Surjit bought a spacious house in the same area where they had once lived. After a prayer ceremony at the gurdwara, Surjit and Karam moved into their new home.

The Covid-19 pandemic continued to take a toll on people all over the world. Especially hit by the virus were Brazil, Italy, Spain, France and the US. All these countries declared lockdown and stay-at-home orders to try and contain the pandemic. Surjit got orders from abroad, and he employed more manpower to work three shifts a day to meet those orders.

Kuljit, too, got infected with Covid-19 in New York, which was hit hard by the pandemic. Amarjit was also infected. Hospitals were stretched to the limit, and there were vaccine shortages everywhere. Honey and Bunty knocked on every door for help, but to no avail. The system was breaking down; there were restrictions everywhere.

That was when Bunty stumbled upon an article in a newspaper

that claimed that an eighty-year-old Indian entrepreneur named Surjit Singh was manufacturing sanitizers and ventilators that were of top quality and up to USFDA standards. He realized that this was none other than his father, whom he had not called in a very long time. Now he made several frantic calls to Surjit, asking him to help save the life of his wife and his brother-in-law. They were in need of the medicine that he manufactured. Time was of the essence; anything could happen to Amarjit and Kuljit. At first, Surjit refused to oblige, but when his wife intervened, he called the hospital where Kuljit and Amarjit had been admitted. He sent cartons of medicine and vaccine and asked the hospital to treat this as a donation. He wanted the treatment of his relatives to be a priority. He sent ventilators especially for Kuljit and Amarjit. Their lives were saved.

Soon after that, Bunty and Honey called their mother, apologizing profusely for their past behaviour and impudence. They also informed her about the well-being of Kuljit and Amarjit. They wanted to reconnect and promised to visit their parents when the pandemic was over. Karam was still talking to her children when Surjit walked into the room. He took the receiver from his wife and disconnected the phone. Speaking in a harsh tone to his wife, Surjeet remarked, 'We may not be as rich as America, but we are human and we care for mankind.'

He paused briefly before adding, 'The idea that America is invincible is a thing of the past. The people there have become so focused on money that they are willing to stoop to any level. Though it may sound harsh, once bitten, twice shy. We should forget and forgive them. They are now Americans, and nothing can change that.'

The telephone began ringing once again, but this time Karam Kaur made no effort to answer it.

THREE

KALPVRIKSH

Manish Chaudhary lay in his hospital bed, staring up at the ceiling fan, which hummed slowly above him. He had overheard that he had a brain tumour which was currently in the fourth stage and had developed to an enormous size of 2.5 cm by 3.5 cm. His sons—Tapan, Som and Jatin—stood in the room, anxiously waiting for the doctor to arrive. Dr Balraj, a physician and an old friend of Manish's, arrived. Tapan, the eldest son who was in his late forties, looked at his siblings before speaking up. 'Doctor, all three of us have come to the realization that we cannot afford to pay the medical bills for our good-for-nothing father. Discharge him immediately so that we can take him home. As it is, he will survive only for a few hours or at most a day or two. What is the point of keeping him here when his condition worsens by the day?'

Dr Balraj looked at the three sons and responded, 'I have just checked his latest reports, and while he may live for over a month, it is unlikely that he will survive much longer than that. So I will advise you to not take him with you.' He paused for a moment and then continued, 'When I entered the room, I heard you people discussing the death of someone who is still alive. That is not good. He is your father, and there was a time when he was revered by millions. I, too, am one of his fans. Dear children, this old man deserves some respect at least. I will advise you to allow a neurosurgeon to operate upon him. If the tumour is removed, he might live longer.'

The potbellied Som moved closer to the doctor and spoke in a menacing voice. He hissed, 'This old man has put us in a pitiable position by churning out one flop film after another. We are in heavy debts and can barely make ends meet. Let's not discuss ethics. Please discharge him so that we can take him home. We will not hold you or the hospital responsible for his demise.' Jatin intervened, 'Enough is enough, doctor sahib. We can't live in the past and bask in those glorious days. Nobody even looks at him. No one is bothered whether he lives or not. Because of him, our lives are no better than garbage in a trash can. We can't pay for the operation, and there is no guarantee that the operation will be successful. Can you give us a guarantee that he will survive the operation at this stage?' Dr Balraj replied, 'No doctor can give a guarantee...but there is a chance.' Jatin cut him short, 'No Sir, we are not taking any chances. Forget about the operation and discharge him today itself.'

'Well, if that is what you all wish, give me a few hours to get clearances from the various departments and organize the paperwork,' Dr Bhattacharya replied. 'But you will need to sign a form stating that the decision to take him home is yours and that you will bear complete responsibility.' Jatin replied, 'Oh yes, Sir, we shall not hold you or the hospital responsible for anything that happens to him.'

Chaudhary, the frail and helpless man lying on the hospital bed, was writhing in pain. He had been given a heavy dose of painkillers, but the pain was still unbearable. He was seventy-six years old, had marginally lost his hearing, and his vision in one eye had been rapidly deteriorating over the last few months. He was in a hopeless condition, both physically and financially. Once a stalwart of the Indian film industry, he was one of its brightest lights, commanding admiration, awe and respect. Robust and handsome, he used to attract everyone's attention. That man was now a liability, and his future was in the hands of his calculating sons. He would soon be discharged from Nanavati Hospital, Mumbai, not because he could not be treated, but because his sons were unwilling to pay any more hospital bills. Though the sons barely spoke to each other, they had taken the unanimous decision to spend no more money on their father and let him die. The senior surgeon had said that the expensive surgery to remove his tumour would not be possible without the money for the hospital expenses.

Apart from his three sons, Manish had a daughter, Priya, who lived in Bangalore. She was married to a computer engineer who had a junior position at Microsoft. Manish lived in a house in Chembur, Mumbai. Though the house had six rooms and a large kitchen, it was in a dilapidated condition. The worn-out furniture, broken railings and shattered window panes spoke of a family that had once known better times but had now fallen on hard times. Due to financial difficulties, frequent quarrels erupted among the family members.

Although his senses were shutting down one by one, Manish's mind was as agile as ever. His mind took a trip down memory lane. He recalled his early days, when he worked as a peon-cum-cook at a university in Bengal. He closed his eyes and it all came flooding back as if he was watching the movie of his life on a 70 mm screen. He smiled and murmured to himself, 'An old, beleaguered wolf is but food for his pups. Repentance and regrets will not change my recent past and happenings. Oh, Nandini, why did you leave me so early in life? When you went to heaven, you took everything with you—my Midas touch, my creativity, all of it.' His brain had gone into a flashback.

In the 1940s, a nine-year-old Manish was playing with his cousins in the small alleys of Calcutta. His father was a schoolteacher who always emphasized the importance of studying—something Manish constantly resisted. No one realized that his aversion to studies was partly due to undiagnosed dyslexia. Instead, he was passionately creative, but that didn't matter much in a family that valued academic education above all things. At the age of thirteen, Manish failed his exams. His father had beaten him black and blue. Manish had contemplated running away from home several times.

When new movie theatres began screening films, Manish developed an obsessive passion for them. Even at a very young age, he intuitively knew that his future lay in the world of films. But how would that happen? His family was financially at its lowest ebb. India was in a period of great transition as Gandhi's Quit India movement was reaching a climax. The British were under pressure to leave the country, and Manish's father, a freedom fighter to the core, had been put in jail. Whatever little money was coming into the house had also dried up. His mother, Aparna, took up embroidery work. They could barely make ends meet. His father, who was put behind bars for participating in the freedom struggle, was an inspiring figure. His mother, the epitome of love, tried to instil in him good values. She would narrate the epic Ramayana to him. Manish dreamed of growing up and becoming a successful businessman so he could provide his mother with all the worldly luxuries.

Manish, driven by his passion for films but seeing no opportunity for it, ran away from home while his father was still in prison. He took up a job as a peon at Rabindranath Tagore's Visva-Bharati University. One day while serving tea, he came into contact with D. Roy. He began to listen in on discussions related to film and film making courses being taught at university by D. Roy. He was fascinated by the ideas on film making being discussed and propounded by D. Roy.

Roy once told him, 'Manish, what makes a sword valuable is the hand that holds it. Otherwise, it's just another piece of craftsmanship. Similarly, a camera or a film is valuable depending upon the director who directs it.'

At the university, Manish took on various odd jobs, including being a peon, assistant cook and washerman. He never said no to anything his employers wanted. He was sharp and hardworking and could connect with people easily, even those who were years older than him. He worked at the university for many years, learning the art of cooking and cleaning. But more than anything, he learned the art of charming anyone he came into contact with.

He continued to watch films whenever he could. By the time he was twenty-three, he was spending almost all his money watching the films that were screened in Calcutta, even the C-grade ones. At some point, he gathered courage and approached D. Roy for a job in his film unit. He was willing to do any kind of errand he was given. Seeing his enthusiasm, Roy hired him as an odd-job man for his film. It was 1954 and Manish was on the set every day, watching every move and the direction that Roy gave. And without formal education or formal training of any kind, Manish learned the art of film-making under one of cinema's greatest directors.

He worked hard and learned fast. Before long, Roy promoted him to the position of assistant director. Sooner than expected, he had mastered several aspects of film-making, and now his suggestions were being taken seriously even by Roy. But Manish was ambitious. He realized that he could make more money in commercial cinema than art films. It was time to leave Calcutta and move to Tinseltown. Bombay was a land of opportunities for talented people like him.

In the early sixties, Manish moved to Bombay. Even amidst the glitz and glamour of the film world, he never forgot his mother. He dutifully sent her five hundred rupees every month. It was all he could afford after paying for his living expenses. In Bombay, Manish joined the film unit of the great film-maker and showman Shri Sashadhar Mukherjee, a highly respected producer who had co-produced the film *Anand Math*, which had gone on to receive a lot of critical acclaim at various international festivals. He had joined the film unit as an errand boy. Most of the time, he was asked to do the work of a clapper or a gaffer. Once he made a suggestion to the director that offended him and resulted in his expulsion from the studio. Despite the setback, Mukherjee was impressed by Manish's passion and offered him the directorship of his new venture. Manish got his first break as a director in a film starring the handsome Joy Mukherjee and the beautiful actress Asha Parekh. The film turned out to be a superhit.

As time passed, Manish developed his unique film making style. In the beginning, he directed a few films for his mentor, guide and philosopher. Though the films became superhits, they were formula films. Later, he formed his own production house under the banner Aparna International, named after his mother. Driven by a desire to succeed, he worked tirelessly. In the sixties and early seventies, his production house churned out one commercial hit after another, starring all the top heroes of the day, including Dev Anand, Joy Mukherjee, Shammi Kapoor, Biswajit and Rajesh Khanna.

Though he had moved out of Filmalaya Studio, owned by Sashadhar Mukherjee, he always remembered what the thespian filmmaker had told him, 'Manish, do you know which is the biggest room? It is the room for improvement. Keep improving the quality of your films and the audience will adore your work.'

While working under the banner of Filmalaya, Manish had

become friends with Romi Chatterjee, who also hailed from Calcutta and was a nephew of Sashadhar Mukherjee. Romi would often incorporate Manish's valuable suggestions into his scripts. However, Romi eventually left for America and settled there, once and for all.

By now, Manish had brought his mother from Calcutta. He handed over the keys to his newly constructed bungalow in Chembur to her. There was an army of servants ready to do her bidding. The bad days that his mother had lived through, often without a penny in the house, were now a thing of the past.

Manish became so successful that Raj Kapoor, the super-showman of the film industry, once remarked, 'I have learned the art of film making from stalwarts such as V. Shantaram, but I have learned "what to make" from Manish Chaudhary.' Raj Kapoor said that Manish was both a man with a vision and a heart of gold—a man who had his finger on the pulse of the audience. All the top stars wanted to work with Manish and were willing to give him any dates he wanted. Dilip Kumar, Manoj Kumar, Rajendra Kumar, Rajesh Khanna and Joy Mukherjee all queued up outside his door.

Manish had the golden touch. Everything he made was a success. Money was pouring in from everywhere. It was a giddy time, and he stood at the pinnacle of his success. No one even called him by his name anymore. He was known simply as the 'Showman' or 'The Doyen of the Film Industry'.

There was nothing Manish wanted that he could not have had. His mother, whose health was deteriorating, began urging him to get married. Manish could have proposed to any beauty queen, who would have gladly accepted him. He could have married the heroine of one of his films. Instead, he chose a sweet and simple woman who had starred in a sister's role in one of his films. Nandini was beautiful and innocent, a combination that Manish found very appealing. She was Bengali and only twenty-one years old, sixteen years younger than him. She had accepted his marriage proposal with great joy. Their wedding reception at the Sun & Sand Hotel in Juhu, Mumbai, became the event of the year with all the top figures in the film industry in attendance.

Top heroes like Joy Mukherjee—who starred as a romantic hero in many films and who was earning upwards of ten lakh rupees per film at that time—were willing to work with Manish for a lower fee.

Manish was at the zenith of his career, and everything was going extremely well. His wife usually accompanied him to all outdoor locations and devoted herself to fulfilling his desires and needs. She had given up on her acting career to support her husband, who had an ocean of talent. Manish was so busy with work that he could not handle his finances by himself. His wife suggested that he bring in her brother, Jagdish, to take care of all his finances. The couple had three sons by that time, all of whom were admitted to St Peter's School in Panchgani. They also had a daughter, Priya, who was the youngest child. She was as beautiful and docile as her mother. She remained with her parents and was admitted to Bombay Scottish School. She also travelled with her parents on outdoor film shootings and quickly became the darling of the entire film unit.

Money was rolling in like never before, and Manish was on a buying spree. He bought flats in Juhu and Carter Road in Bombay; Mount Road in Bangalore; and Connaught Place in New Delhi. He also made a state-of-the-art film studio, Nandini Studios, at Juhu Tara Road, which he named after his beloved wife. It was inaugurated with a level of fanfare seldom seen before. Amitabh Bachchan gave the first shot and Manish's closest friend, Joy Mukherjee, gave the first clap.

By the age of thirty-seven, Manish won a prestigious award for his directorial venture *Soar as High as Possible*.

And then everything came crashing down like a pack of cards.

Sixteen years after their marriage, Nandini, who was by now thirty-eight, was diagnosed with a life-threatening disease. She had a hole in her heart. She did not have long to live. The news devastated Manish. He abandoned the film he was working on midway, left his finances for Jagdish to handle, and flew his ailing wife to St George's Hospital in London. He devoted all his time, money and energy to care for his wife.

His well-wishers warned him not to leave all financial control with his brother-in-law, who was known to gamble and was often seen at the Mahalaxmi Race Course. His eldest son, now fifteen, also advised his father against relying so much on his uncle, but Manish was too preoccupied with his wife's illness and was unwilling to listen to anyone. Manish informed everyone that Nandini was recuperating and feeling much better in London, and that he would stay there as long as necessary. He believed that Jagdish would never betray his sister and brother-in-law.

For three years, he nursed Nandini in London. He took her to every specialist in the city. He intuitively knew that his presence made her feel better so he never left her side. But life had other plans. Nandini's health kept deteriorating and after a prolonged illness, she was gone. She passed away in the hospital after being in a coma for two months. Manish was shattered.

By the time Manish returned to Bombay, everything had changed. His unscrupulous brother-in-law had siphoned off a large portion of his money. Several people from his production house had taken jobs elsewhere. Manish still tried to regain his foothold in the industry, relying on his reputation as the doyen of the film world. He sold off some of his properties to try and make a comeback film. Unfortunately, it bombed at the box office. He tried again, mortgaging other properties to make another film with a popular star. That too failed miserably. Bankers moved in and auctioned his flats at Juhu and Carter Road. Manish tried a third time, this time mortgaging the Chembur house they were living in, to make his most ambitious multi-starrer film. That too bombed at the box office. He was neck-deep in loans and had no means left to repay them.

The dream run was over. He had lost his golden touch and along with it, his fortune and assets. Manish was practically living on the roadside at that point. The debts were piling up. Those who had once been his friends and admirers deserted him. Top film stars, who had once queued up at his door, no longer wanted to work with him. He switched to making B-grade films, but nothing Manish made seemed to work anymore. He was alone in his studio and eventually that was sold off too.

In the three years that he was away, he had aged by ten years. Without Nandini, his life had little meaning. Meanwhile, there were debts to be paid and bankers were unrelenting. One by one, his cars were sold off. Ultimately, the great showman was reduced to taking a job as an assistant director to a new upcoming director, but that didn't work out either. His feedback on a particular scene was not appreciated, and he was let go on the same day. He turned to his close friend Bharat Bhushan for financial help, but to no avail. Even Bharat was facing a crisis and had been forced to sell his house to jubilee star Rajendra Kumar.

As the days passed and people began avoiding him, Manish became more and more of a recluse. His sons could not complete their studies and took up menial jobs. Som was as tall as Manish, and although he did not complete his graduation, he was street smart and became an insurance agent. Jatin joined a private firm as a salesman. Tapan worked as an accountant with a film production company, a job he got on purely sympathetic grounds. Somehow, they managed to scrape through and continue to live in their own house. Priya, his daughter, got married to a computer engineer and now lived in Bangalore with her two school-going daughters. The three sons of the doyen developed a complex that engulfed their life. They were always measured against their father's numerous accomplishments. Despite their good looks and pleasing personalities, the frequent comparisons with their father and being labelled 'good for nothing' had distanced them from Manish.

In better times, Manish had helped many people. It was well-known in the industry that anyone who knocked on Manish's door never went away disappointed. He would often hand out lakhs of rupees to those in need. But now, years had passed and no one bothered about the ace director any more. His house, which was once a pilgrimage centre, always full of flowers and gifts sent by admirers, was now deserted and dilapidated. No more heroes and heroines walking in and begging to star in his films. No more security guards waiting outside the main gate. No more flashy cars crowding the driveway. The house at Chembur was in ruins. And here he was, the doyen of the film industry, lying helplessly in a hospital bed. He was waiting for the inevitable to happen—death and relief from all the troubles.

Manish was lost in his thoughts when someone touched his hand. An old friend had come to visit him in the hospital. 'What a pleasant surprise,' Manish managed to speak with great difficulty. 'You have taken the trouble to come all the way to meet me, and here are my three sons who want me dead. I never thought I would see the day when my children would want to get rid of me. I am a burden on them.' A tear silently rolled down his cheek. The old friend held Manish's hand and they talked for a while. The friend reflected on the cruel twist of fate that had brought Manish to this state. He wasn't sure he would see him alive again. Manish smiled with a tinge of pain in his eyes and said, 'Dear friend, I am in a miserable condition, both in term of health and finances. Even my sons do not want to support me. In the history of mankind, money is the worst invention with the power to cause catastrophe. But it is also true that money is the most effective tool to assess the true nature and character of a person.' After a while, the friend left, realizing that Manish was in the final stages of his life.

The same afternoon, Manish was reluctantly discharged by Dr Balraj on the insistence of his sons. He was shifted to a makeshift room in his Chembur house. A few days passed in pain. Manish knew his life was fading fast. His daughter had come from Bangalore to take care of him. Barely able to speak now, he signalled to her that he wanted to see some photographs of Nandini. He had sensed that he had only a few moments to live and wanted to take one last look at his beloved wife.

Unlike her brothers, Priya was devoted to her father. She was only five when her parents left for London for medical treatment, and she was eight when her mother passed away. Priya had only faint memories of her mother. However, everyone said she strongly resembled her, not only in looks but also in mannerisms. As father and daughter looked at the albums together, the photographs spoke of better days and the phenomenal success Manish had once enjoyed—a showman who was once without any parallel in the film industry. There was the photo of Manish winning the coveted Dadasaheb Phalke Award and another of him winning the Filmfare Award. The album contained countless pages of awards given to Manish, with Nandini always by his side. Manish kept the album aside and closed his eyes. Priya wept uncontrollably, holding her father's hand, while her three brothers fidgeted impatiently in the room. Manish lost consciousness, and for some time, it looked as if he was gone.

Manish regained consciousness but his vision was blurry. He could make out that his sons and daughter were standing close by, and a doctor was trying to revive him. Manish wanted to tell the doctor to stop, but his body was inert. No words came out of his mouth. His soul was slowly leaving his body. Taking one last look at his children and grandchildren surrounding him, the once-celebrated doyen of the film industry passed into another world.

❧

After cleansing his remains, the body was kept in the main hall so that relatives and friends could have their last *darshan*. Two junior reporters from the Press Trust of India came to cover his demise, although they were unsure whether anyone would be interested in reading about a has-been. They came because they were told to do the story. By afternoon, several relatives and some friends had turned up to pay their last respects to the departed soul. The silence in that dimly lit hall was suddenly broken when Manish's old friend Ramnath, also known as Romi, walked in dramatically. He bellowed, 'You cannot perform the last rites till my loan of five crore rupees has been repaid.' All eyes turned to Romi, who was a close friend of Manish and had been living in America for the past twenty years.

There was shocked silence. What was Romi saying? What loan? And, how could he speak so harshly at such an emotional moment? Romi raised his voice once more, saying, 'Give me my money. I have a court order with me. You cannot perform any rites till my loan is paid back.'

Jatin rose from a corner of the hall and rushed to Romi. He pleaded with him to not raise his voice and behave so indecently at such a delicate time. Everyone knew they had no money and could not raise even five lakh rupees, let alone five crore. But Romi was unrelenting. He had come with two lawyers and three police inspectors. He pulled out the court order which gave him the right to recover his money. He wanted to take possession of the house which was already mortgaged for three crore rupees and was soon to be auctioned by bankers. He held the high court decree as evidence of the loan given and his right to reclaim his funds from the only estate of Manish's 'Chaudhary Mansion'.

Som and Tapan arrived at Romi's side, imploring him not to execute the decree. However, Romi was adamant, saying, 'I'm sorry but I will not let you proceed with the last rites till my money has been paid back. After all, it was my hard-earned money that was given to Manish as a temporary loan. I never gifted it to him. Now I have full right to reclaim it.'

Som was distraught, saying, 'Uncle, you have been a friend of our father's. We don't recall him ever taking a loan from you or what happened to that money—if he, in fact, borrowed such a huge sum from you.'

Romi would not listen. 'I have court orders,' he said. 'I have paid the lawyers a lot of money to obtain this decree. Either you repay my loan immediately and then proceed with the last rites or vacate this house in accordance with the court order. Everything here belongs to me. I have a right to this property and everything in this house,' he asserted.

'Uncle, we can barely make ends meet,' Tapan said bluntly. 'How on earth can we repay this debt? Our father has passed away, and his debts are no longer our responsibility. We know our father was under heavy debt and might have taken this loan from you, but how are we supposed to repay it?'

'My dear Tapan, you do not know the law. You are naive. A loan taken by the parents becomes the legal responsibility of the children to repay since they, too, have benefitted from that money,' Romi said in a sharp voice.

'Sir, please do not create a scene here,' Som pleaded. 'There are relatives and press reporters around. Everything will get reported tomorrow. The papers will accuse our father of taking a huge loan and frittering it away on a flop film. Please spare him that.'

Romi retorted, 'I don't give a damn about what your relatives think or what the press says. I want my money and that's it. I didn't come from the US for anything else. Just pay me my money and I will leave with these policemen and lawyers. Otherwise, vacate this house right now, and I will auction it and recover my money. I thank my stars that I came to India in time and have received the orders from the judge.'

Tapan responded with folded hands, the self-righteousness now leaving his voice, 'Uncle please, for old times' sake, please let us discuss this matter amongst ourselves.' Finally, Romi, while shrugging his shoulders, conceded to this request.

The house was swarming with inquisitive relatives. The brothers got together in a corner and tried to assess the situation. Being the eldest, Tapan took charge. 'How dare this man barge in and create a scene?' he said angrily. 'Did either of you have any idea about this loan? Is this the principal amount or has he added interest? I can't leave the house just like that.' He then confessed that there were some antiques and paintings which the others didn't know about and some jewellery he had hidden in his almirah in case of any crisis. Now he was panicking. 'If Romi forces us to vacate this house immediately, he may take those valuables too. They are worth at least thirty lakh rupees. And, according to the court order, he says everything in the house also belongs to him. I must confess that I have taken all this from father without informing you people.'

Tapan butted in, 'What kind of a person are you? You've

hidden valuables and jewellery and never told us. That's not fair. We were struggling to pay medical bills, and you have stowed away valuables worth thirty lakh rupees. Are you insane?'

'What could I do?' Tapan replied. 'Father asked me to sell or mortgage these things, but my wife insisted that we lock them in the cupboard and use them for Minnie's marriage. I gave some money to my father against the valuables from my own earnings. That jewellery, in a way, now belongs to me.'

Som piped in, 'That's pure misappropriation. You have no right to keep everything for yourself. Even I have a daughter, and I will need jewellery and money for her wedding someday. Oh my God! I never expected my elder brother to act like a thief. You have stolen expensive items of the family.' Tapan retorted, 'Shut up! I have not stolen the items but paid for them.' Som taunted, 'Paid what? Peanuts?'

Now, with the threat of everything being discovered and taken from them, Som confessed that he, too, had approximately seven lakh rupees of cash in his almirah. 'But that is the insurance company's money and not mine,' he justified. 'One day, I intend to return it. I have been using the money for teeming and lading.'

'What do you mean by that?' asked Jatin. 'I have never come across such terms.'

Som replied, 'Teeming and lading means taking company funds, using it to pay for insurance, and then when the money comes, it goes directly into the person's account whose name is marked as a nominee on the policy. In the company records, the amount is shown as outstanding.'

'Ah, you pretended to have no money to pay our father's medical bills, and all along you had seven lakh stashed away in your almirah,' said Tapan.

Mutual suspicion rose among the brothers, but there was no time for squabbling and finger-pointing. There was the very real fear of losing all their worldly possessions to Romi. Tapan continued, 'I think we should forget about our father's last rites and just take all our valuables and leave the house through the back door. Else, that greedy man from the US may take everything we have. Come, let's vamoose and keep the money and valuables at a safe place.'

Som agreed with Tapan, and they decided to quickly discuss the matter with their wives. They planned to run away with the possessions before they were compelled to hand over everything to Romi. 'To hell with Father's last rites and to hell with the house, which now has two claimants—the bank and Uncle Romi,' Tapan muttered, cursing his father. It was a complete mess as even the builder, who had advanced them some money, had a stake in the property.

Tapan said, 'No one knows that we have entered into a collaboration agreement with Ranjit Singh Bedi and taken 10 per cent from him. I cannot repay the builder now. Let's forget about Ranjit Singh Bedi for the time being. Let's concentrate on how to handle this situation.'

By this time, Romi sensed something was amiss. He sent the police to fetch the brothers as they were about to escape with the valuables and cash from the back door. They were caught and brought back into the living room.

Priya, who had been quietly observing the scene, spoke for the first time. 'Romi Uncle, my father always spoke highly of you, and here you are, creating a scene at such an emotional time when we are all gathered to offer our prayers. Could you please tell us when he took this money from you?'

Romi's voice softened a bit. 'Ah, you're Priya, aren't you? I saw you last when you were perhaps eight years old. It's all written in the court order—the dates, cheque numbers and the bank from which the loan was given. Everything is given in this detailed decree. Why don't you go through it? The court passed this order after deliberating on the issue.'

'So it may be, Uncle,' she said. 'But I can't let my father's body lie here just like that. Could you please give my brothers and me some time to talk in private?'

Romi granted Priya's request, saying, 'All right, I will give you people ten minutes. And that too because of you, Priya, and your concern for your father—but not a minute more.' Raising his voice, he said, 'And remember that I am not leaving without getting what is owed to me.

Romi went back to the hall and joined his lawyers. By this time, all the visitors who had come to pay their last respects were absorbed in the family drama unfolding before their eyes. They spoke in loud whispers. 'Yes,' agreed another, 'he probably took loan after loan to make films that just kept flopping.' The bellyaching and gossiping continued unabated.

In the adjoining room, Priya pleaded with her elder brothers, 'We must all get together and return the money which our father owed Romi Uncle. If he auctions this house, nothing will be left. Even the nameplate, 'Chaudhary Mansion', will be wiped out forever. You will have to find someplace else to live. Please let's all contribute and pay him some money now so that we can calm him down for a little while and proceed with the last rites of our dear father.'

'Are you out of your mind Priya?' said an enraged Som. 'To hell with Romi Uncle and his decree. I will obtain a stay order from the court, but I refuse to contribute even a single penny. We can barely meet our expenses. Where the hell do you think we could find money to give Romi? Is it going to fall from the skies? You must be crazy to think of repaying even five lakh to that man.'

Priya pleaded again, her hands folded. 'Please brothers, we can sell the rights of some old films of Aparna International to

distributors. I am sure someone will buy them. These days, all
the old films are being shown on hundreds of TV channels. Then
your wives probably have some jewellery that we can give to Romi
Uncle. I have a fixed deposit of twenty lakh in my daughter's
name in Bangalore. I can get that encashed and give it to him.
If we try, we can salvage the situation.'

Now Som intervened. 'You are insane, Priya,' he said. 'You
look like our mother, but you lack her intelligence. I don't have
any bonds or fixed deposits that I can encash. My employers are
already hinting that they will fire me for not having achieved my
sales targets. Do not expect anything from my side. Our father
sold our mother's jewellery to pay for those flopped films as well
as his medical treatment. And as for expecting our wives to give
away their jewellery, you must be out of your mind. My wife
could hardly tolerate the crazy old man. I do not have the guts
to ask her to part with her jewellery.'

Now, it was Jatin's turn. 'I am still unmarried at thirty-four
because no one wants to marry his daughter to a vagabond like
me,' he said. 'You think I have any money to spare? People who
made millions of rupees off our father have not even bothered
to come and pay their last respects. Do you see anyone in that
hall of any stature? No, they're all making fun of us and enjoying
the downfall of our family. Please don't expect anything from
me either.'

Priya turned to Tapan with hopeful eyes. Tapan rose from
his chair, paused, and said, 'Priya, we love you but you must
understand the miseries that our father brought into our lives.
He gave us nothing but a life full of litigation and insults. You
have no idea how humiliating it was for me to sell our silver and
gold items, one after the other, to pay the lawyers just to prevent
the banks from taking over this house. This is all we have and we
will not leave this house, come what may. Romi Uncle can go to

hell. He is not a good man. He's a scheming, greedy scoundrel.'

'Who's calling me a scoundrel?' yelled Romi as he entered the room. 'I've been waiting for a long time, and it seems you people have no intention to repay the money you owe me. It's time for me to execute the decree and kick all of you out of this house.'

'But, Uncle, where will we go?' said Jatin in a state of panic. Romi retorted, 'That's not my problem. I will make sure you people are on the streets and have nothing to do with this house or its belongings. From now on, everything belongs to me,' he declared vehemently.

He turned to Tapan, 'Already this house has a liability of three crore rupees. It's not even worth the five crore you people owe me, is it Tapan?'

Priya came forward, her hands folded, 'Uncle, please give us some more time, we will repay you. Rather, I undertake the responsibility to repay the loan my father took from you. Uncle, please bear with us at this sad moment and the trauma we are going through.' She took off her jewellery and handed it to Romi, saying, 'Uncle, for now, please keep this jewellery, which is worth five or six lakh rupees, and the same shall reveal my intention to repay your debt. I also have a fixed deposit, a car and some more jewellery that I had kept aside for my daughters' wedding. I will turn all that over to you. Please, please allow us to perform our father's last rites, and do not throw my brothers out of the house. They have nowhere to go. Tapan and Som have wives and little children. Where will they go, Uncle?'

Romi was unrelenting. He now spoke in a voice loud enough to be heard in the hall outside. 'Nothing doing, Priya. I want my money now. I already have symbolic possession of the house through the court decree. Now I will take physical possession too.' His voice emphasized the word 'possession'. 'I want it and I will have it, come what may.'

Tapan could take it no longer. He unleashed his anger, 'First my brother said you are a scoundrel, and now I shall say it too. You are a scoundrel of the highest order. You may have made it big in the US, but you have no decency, etiquette or manners. You are a man without any feelings for your friend, whose body is lying outside. We are poor and cannot match your wealth, but that does not mean we will give in to you. I will go to the high court and obtain a stay order against that goddamn decree that you are flaunting so shamelessly. I will see you in court, you unscrupulous man.'

'Ah, so it is I who is unscrupulous and not you?' Romi mimicked Tapan. 'Who claimed to have no money for medical bills? That's what you said to Dr Balraj. You were willing to let your father die? All the while you were sitting on a secret stash of money. Does anyone talk with so much disrespect about a great man like your father? Was that me? No, let me remind you of the words you used with the doctor, "Let the old, stupid man die. He does not deserve to live anymore." That is what you said about your father, and that is why he was discharged without proper medical treatment.'

Priya was stunned by this. 'Brother, what is this? Did you tell the doctor to stop life support and withdraw treatment? Why? He may have lived for a few days or even a month. This was not fair on your part.'

'Sister, we had no money,' Tapan replied and then quickly threw the accusations back at Romi. 'And look at this rogue who, on one hand, claims that our father was a great man and, on the other, insults his family and does not even allow us to proceed with the great man's last rites.'

Romi smiled, 'Sure, I am a rogue no doubt but tell me, who was at the Mahalaxmi Race Course last Sunday betting on horses? All the while your father was fighting for his life, you were out at the race course gambling. What a great son you've been to your illustrious father. Whether you had money or no money, you should have shown respect for the old man. I am only two years younger than him, but I revered him for his genius and generosity. It was not his fault that your mother had a terminal illness, and he had to spend years looking after her. It was not his doing that his brother-in-law, your maternal uncle, betrayed him and siphoned off his money and spent it on the races and gambling. Instead of following in the footsteps of your noble father, you've gone the way of your wicked uncle instead. You people do not deserve to be the great man's sons.'

Romi now turned to Som, 'And you Som, you pretend to be very upright when you claim you will return the money you secretly took from your office. And you plead for sympathy saying you may be retrenched. The truth is you have embezzled at least ten lakh from the insurance premiums you received in cash from the policyholders. For sure, you will not only be retrenched but also be put behind bars for stealing and misappropriation of funds. And yes, I know too that you have been squandering money and spending lavishly on alcohol and your friends.'

Priya looked at her brother in shock. Jatin exclaimed in surprise, 'But it is me who is supposed to be the black sheep of the family. Som would never do such a thing. He would never embezzle money and use it to throw lavish parties for his friends. I do not have money and have not been able to get married due to a paucity of funds. I shall die a bachelor.'

'Really?' Romi said sarcastically. 'Then what about the dancer from the bar who you took to Mahabaleshwar last month where you spent three nights in Mount View Hotel in room number 314? All the while, you told your brothers that you were on a business tour. It was only your father who was devoted to his wife, who was a true one-woman man. Your father was in a position where he could have asked any woman to spend the night with him and she would have readily obliged. But no, he was a man of principle, faithful to his wife unto his last breath.'

'Priya, these brothers of yours have entered into an agreement to sell this house to the builder Ranjit Singh Bedi. What happened to the advance money that he gave the three of you four months ago?'

The brothers stood with their mouths open. Where had Romi Uncle been getting all this information? The gathered relatives were tuning in to his every word, hardly able to believe what was going on. Priya said, 'Uncle, my brothers are emotionally disturbed. We must repay your loan. I humbly request you to let us perform his last rites. I take responsibility for your loan. I may take time to repay it since it is a large amount. But even if I have to take a job somewhere, I promise to repay my father's debt. I will not let his name be tarnished. I have loved him, and I will honour his memory.' She started to weep inconsolably.

'How much time will you take?' roared Romi, 'And what about the money that they owe to the builder?'

Priya replied, tears flowing from her eyes. 'It may take a year, maybe even more than that, Romi Uncle. Two things are clear. My brothers are not going to contribute anything, and I will have to dispose of whatever I have. But I will do whatever I have to do to repay you. I shall repay the loan even if I have to sell my furniture. I will also reply to the builder whosoever he may be. Please do not ask them to vacate this house.'

Romi cautioned, 'Priya, do not promise what you cannot deliver. Remember, during the journey of life, never ever give a response when you are angry, never give a boon when in a pleasurable mood, and never take any decision when you are extremely tense, unhappy or emotionally charged.'

Som butted in, 'Priya, are you crazy? How on earth are you

going to come up with five crore rupees? Let this vicious man, who is as stupid as our father, try and take over this house. We will fight back. We will not surrender in any way. He will get this house over my dead body. I will show him the stuff I am made of. Priya, you go to the living room and let us deal with this rogue of a man. Americans have no sentiments. They breathe, eat and sleep with bloody dollars only. I will see this man and teach him a lesson or two.'

'Ah, so you will fight me from prison, will you?' mocked Romi. 'You are facing at least five years behind bars, my dear. And do you have the money to pay lawyers to fight a legal battle? When notices were sent for the recovery of five crore rupees, why didn't you acknowledge them? How else could I get ex-parte orders from the court? Now you want a court battle with me? You are the one who is *crazy*, not her.'

Priya reprimanded her brother. 'Som, please apologize for your rudeness. Don't call him names. I do not know the reason for Romi Uncle being so harsh with us, but he is still our elder and a family friend. We should not be disrespectful to him.'

But Jatin was in no mood to calm down. 'Does it look like this man has ever been a friend to our father?' he said. 'He is just a greedy man who has always had an eye on our house. I know these Americans will die for money. I do not know from where or how you have landed up with this decree. But I will fight it till my last breath.'

Priya appealed to Jatin, 'We will reach nowhere if we go on like this. Everyone sitting outside who came to pay their last respects to our father is now gossiping.' She turned to Romi, 'Uncle, please take all of my jewellery and my car keys. There are also some antiques lying in the storeroom. Please take them too for whatever they are worth. The rest I promise to pay you even if I have to beg, borrow or steal. Please, Uncle, it's getting late and as per Hindu rites, we cannot light the funeral pyre after dark. Please allow us to proceed.' By that time, Priya was weeping uncontrollably.

'Your attitude is baffling, Uncle,' Tapan intervened. 'On one hand, you behave like a greedy and ruthless moneylender, ready to usurp our only asset, which is this house. On the other hand, you call our father a great genius and ask us to talk about him with respect. We are confused. And how could you know such minute details of what we've been doing in the past? Everything about you baffles me.'

Romi said, 'Well, I do not owe you any explanation. I want my money and the matter ends there. Arrange for at least one crore right now, and I will leave. You shall have a month to pay the remaining amount.'

Tapan simmered down a bit and pleaded, 'Uncle give us some more time to talk it out with our wives. We shall be back with you in ten minutes or so. Priya, even you excuse us.'

Romi said, 'Not even a second more than ten minutes.' He, along with Priya, left for the living room. They noticed that all the relatives hurriedly went back to their places.

The brothers decided to take out the expensive items, money and jewellery from the cupboards and escape from the back door. They collected their belongings and ran towards the back door, only to find the lawyer and the police waiting for them along with Romi.

Romi said, 'I knew you would do something like this.'

Tapan retorted, 'Romi, let us go. These goods and items have nothing to do with our father. It is our self-acquired property and you cannot touch it. I will see you in court.'

Suddenly, Romi did a complete turnaround. 'Tapan, you are not just confused, you are also very foolish. You haven't even asked to see the court order I have been talking about all this while. Had you seen it, you would have realized it's fake. The court decree is fake, the lawyers are also fake and the policemen accompanying me are fake as well. They are all actors from a drama company, masquerading as lawyers and policemen.'

Everyone in the rear courtyard was shocked to hear this. Priya was the first to speak, 'Romi Uncle, why did you play this cruel prank on us at such a time? Didn't you know my father would have felt very disturbed by this? Is this the time to gather actors who can masquerade as lawyers and policemen? Why did you create all this drama, and what made you stoop so low and play with emotions? My father, God bless his soul, would be upset wherever he is.'

'No, my dear child,' Romi said gently. 'Your father is probably smiling because this is exactly what he asked me to do when I met him at the hospital three weeks ago on the day he was to be discharged.'

Romi went on to explain his volte-face, his abrupt and complete reversal of position, 'I had not given a loan of five crore to your father. On the contrary, it was your father who had given me a gift of five crore almost twenty years ago. Yes, it was I who was in debt to your father. When I heard about his current state of health and finances, I flew down to India, especially to return the money which he had given me so generously when I was in dire straits. When I went to meet him at the hospital, Dr Bhattacharya said it was unlikely that he would live more than a few days with his brain cancer—but nothing more than that. Your father felt depressed and told me that he could not succeed in his second innings. I remember his words. He had said, "When the winds of life push you backwards and make you feel depressed, that's when you push the hardest till you change the flow and direction of the wind. But alas, my dear friend, however hard I pushed, I could not change the flow of the winds."' Romi Uncle continued,

'Your father had held my hand and said, "These days, it's difficult to have trustworthy friends since most of them are selfish and are with you with the sole intention of extorting money from you."'

He continued, 'At first, your father refused to take the money from me but finally, on my insistence, he asked me to give it to the most deserving heir of his. I promised to fulfil that request and approached my advisor in India, Sunil Kapoor, for a plan. It was Sunil who drafted the fake decree, and it was he who suggested that I get detectives to follow the siblings to ascertain each one's nature, to figure out who was the most deserving and to whom I should deliver this cheque of five crore rupees.'

Saying so, he took out a blank cheque of five crore. The name had not been filled in the cheque. 'The detectives found and reported to me that out of the four of you, only Priya went to the Shree Siddhivinayak Temple to pray for her father's health every morning. Your father had told me, "Romi, you have come at a most opportune time. After a very long time, I feel good. My sorrows and failures turned an arrogant man like me into a humble being who nobody remembers anymore. But it is the faith in people like you which keeps me going." And that is when he confided in me and asked my help to give this cheque to his most deserving heir.' The relatives had all come out and heard everything that was discussed. Pandemonium reigned in the main hall.

Romi ignored them and continued, 'That is when I put all of you to the test by getting some detective to follow you and investigate your actions. After receiving the reports, I wanted to confront you face to face. But on reaching here, I found that my old friend had passed away. I decided to catch you being your true selves. I quickly recruited actors to play the role of lawyers and policemen and put on the show of a cruel moneylender demanding his money back. I was only doing what your father had asked me to do. And only one of you has passed the test of being his most deserving legal heir—Priya. I intend to give the money to you.' He again pulled out the cheque and wrote Priya's name on it and handed it over to her.

Seeing a potential fortune slip away from his grasp, Tapan said, 'You can't do that, Romi Uncle. If my father gave you five crore rupees a long time back, then as per the Indian Succession Act, all four of his children have an equal right to that money. Not just that, we will claim interest at bank rates on that amount which, after twenty years of compounding, will make your debt at least fifteen to sixteen crore. We will go to court to claim interest and damages from you. As you have admitted, our father gave you the money twenty years ago.'

'Now you will have to pay interest and damages too. I shall see to it that all of us get at least fifteen to sixteen crore out of you,' Som asserted.

Romi Uncle laughed. 'You are both naive and stupid, and will remain so. Honesty and sincerity are expensive virtues. One should never expect them from cheap and short-sighted people like you. Didn't you hear what I said? Your father gave me a gift of five crore, not a loan. He gave it following the rules of the RBI and only after seeking their permission for making the gift. The money was remitted to New York. The RBI form submitted states that this was a gift and not a loan. You cannot invoke the Indian Succession Act on a valid gift made with full documentation by your father. His act is supported by an affidavit where he admits that the gift was made voluntarily and without any undue influence or coercion. I have brought a copy of the requisite affidavit and gift deed for your perusal. These are actual documents and not fake.

'And regarding any interest, I had requested your father to fill in any amount he wanted as interest. I pleaded with him to do so.

I was guilty of getting so involved in setting up my computer disc factory in the US, that over the years, I forgot all about my true friend and benefactor. I asked him to fill in any amount up to twenty crore rupees but he refused. He said, in his heyday when he was rolling in money, he had a policy of never giving loans to friends and relatives. Instead, when someone needed a thousand rupees, he would give him five hundred and then forget all about it. This great man knew that a loan can spoil relationships. Even after becoming penniless, he never called me for financial help. That's the kind of self-respect your father had. Even an amount as huge as five crore that he had gifted me, he forgot about. A long time back, I had asked your father about the crux of life. He had told me on the phone that he had asked the same question from the rising sun. The sun had replied, "Always try and generate more light than heat." You Priya, only you generate light while your brothers generate only heat.

'Do you know what his last words to me were? He said, "My dear friend, you have come in my hour of need as a *kalpvriksh*, the divine tree. I asked him what he meant. He had stated, "Kalpvriksh is a magic tree in Hindu mythology, a tree that can fulfil all your desires. You are a kalpvriksh for me because you can clear my debt without my asking for it. I had been hoping for a miracle to save my name and my house from being auctioned. The thought of Chaudhary Mansion being taken away from the family was causing me great distress. Now you have set my mind to rest, now I can die in peace. Kalpavriksh, that's what you are for me."

'Even if you take birth ten times over, you will never understand your magnanimous father, the great Manish Chaudhary. He was truly unique among men. You brothers can continue to live here but the cheque of five crore will go to his most deserving child, Priya. Tragically, a great man had three sons, but each has a blot on his name. Priya is the only one worthy of his legacy.' He paused and then continued to speak to the spellbound audience.

Romi Uncle smiled and said, 'You don't have to repay any mortgage to the bank. I have already settled with them, and the original sum of two crore rupees paid by the bank has been repaid. The bank will shortly release the original property papers to you. You have no loans on you. Please take this cheque of five crore and treat it as an inheritance from the doyen of the film industry to you. If you want to share it with your brothers, you may do so. After all, they too are the sons of the great showman. And so far as Ranjit Singh Bedi is concerned, here is the receipt for full repayment to him.'

With this, Romi Uncle concluded his statement. The three sons looked down in shame. They had not only misjudged their father but had misjudged Romi Uncle too. They could have honoured their father and learned from him when he was alive. But it was too late now. They had failed miserably on all counts.

Priya walked up to her uncle and hugged him and said, 'Romi Uncle, that was indeed a volte-face. We were all completely taken in by your theatrics. Uncle, I will use this money to pay off all my father's debts so that his soul can rest in peace.'

Priya touched Romi Uncle's feet and walked into the hall where her father's body was lying and asked the priest to perform the last rites. The kalpvriksh had been sent by their father to take them out of all the trouble and save the Chaudhary name for eternity. He turned towards the lifeless body of his true friend and bid farewell to him by quoting a couplet:

Farewell, my dear friend—I can smell your fragrance from close by.
I can feel your demeanor being close to mine.
Know fully well that you shall remain embedded in my heart for a long, long time.

Will cherish the time spent with you.
Will try to make my life sublime.
You may have left me far behind, with your footprints on
the sands of time.
Farewell my friend, farewell.

Priya hugged her brother and coaxed them to touch the feet of
Romi Uncle and apologize for their impudence. She said, 'We
shall all share the legacy of the doyen of the film industry.'

FOUR

YASHO TEJASWINI

Part I

On a quiet night on the rain-washed streets of Mussoorie, the only sound that could be heard was the cool breeze rustling through the mountains. The chilly weather was a reminder that winter had set in. It felt as if the hill station was fast asleep. As the inky darkness spread like a stain, streetlights gleaming in the moist air revealed a lone figure walking silently, using a stick to find his way. He walked slowly, cautiously, relying on his senses to guide him across the bridge on the way to his ancestral home, Shanker Estate, situated in Upper Mall, Kulari, right next to Picture Palace Theatre. Despite being very careful, the man stumbled over a large stone, lost control, rolled over, and fell flat on the road. There was no one to help him get up and show him the way. Neeraj had hurt his knees from the fall, but he got up and kept walking towards his house.

Neeraj was fifteen years old and was born blind. When his mother went into labour, she was diagnosed with severe anaemia. Despite the best efforts of the doctors, they could save only one life between the mother and the child. While Neeraj lived, his mother died on the night he was born, 10 September 1969, at the Civil Hospital in Dehradun.

Neeraj had to fend for himself, relying only on his stick and his active senses to get around. He got hurt when he tripped and fell on the road, but being used to such falls, he quickly recovered and continued his journey home, albeit with more caution. The streetlamps that lit the way made no difference to him. He had no sense of sight. However, his heightened sense of hearing allowed him to detect sounds that an ordinary person might miss out on. He could hear the breeze and even sense that it was blowing in the direction of the mountains at Camel's Back Road. He could hear the soft sounds of the creatures of the night scuttling around in the darkness. He knew the exact number of steps it took him to get from Chic Chocolate to his residence: the eighty-year-old bungalow, Shanker Estate, named after his late and wealthy grandfather, Rai Bahadur Shanker Kapoor. It was a large estate covering five thousand square yards. It consisted of a bungalow—with twenty-six rooms—and outhouses. Located on Upper Mall Road, the estate afforded a stunning view. It was the envy of the residents of Mussoorie.

Neeraj's father was an IAS officer. He had worked hard and had risen to the position of undersecretary at his government job. He was posted at the Central Secretariat in Delhi and had been allotted a spacious Type-V bungalow in Bharti Nagar, near Khan Market. He decided to send Neeraj to Dehradun for two reasons. First, he had close relatives living in Vikas Huts near Rialto Cinema in Mussoorie, who could be the local guardians for his son. Second, and more importantly, the British had established a special boarding school for students who are blind, where they were taught Braille and other coping skills.

His father was well aware that the Doon Valley was one of the first places in India to have a school for students who are blind. Sharp Memorial School for the Blind was established in the early part of the twentieth century and was inaugurated by Lord Wellington in 1935. It was located near the prestigious Doon School and was still the school of choice for people who were visually impaired. After Independence, the Government of India established the Central Braille Press in 1951 and subsequently the National Institute for the Empowerment of Persons with Visual Disabilities (NIVH) in 1967 to support visually impaired people. The Padma Bhushan awardee K.S. Negi had published several books in Braille that were extensively used in Sharp Memorial.

At the moment, Neeraj was spending his vacation in Mussoorie. He had grown into a handsome, athletic man—although he didn't know it himself. As he walked back in the darkness to his house, Neeraj reflected on all that his grandfather had told him about Mussoorie. He remembered vividly what his grandfather had stated, 'My dear Neeraj, the first train from Haridwar had reached Dehradun in 1900, making the Doon Valley more accessible to the rest of India. The Valley's first radio station was launched in the butchery compound in 1899. The telephone came to Mussoorie in 1901 and the television, only in 1975, when the first TV tower was built. And in 1920, according to what a schoolteacher once told him, the first car, a Ford Model T, came to Mussoorie, driven up to Kulri via Jharipani by Colonel E.W. Bell, the son of Swetenhams. By 1930, Mussoorie was built up to Bhatta Fall; by 1936, up to King Craig; and by 1957, it stretched up to Picture Palace.'

Neeraj was one of 89 blind students who, during their school term in Dehradun, stayed in the Sharp Memorial boarding house. Some of the students came from places as far away as Hyderabad and Bombay. There were enough teachers and support staff to help the blind students do their daily chores. It was the third week of the month-long winter holidays, and all the blind students had gone to their homes.

Neeraj had been whiling away his time at his house in Mussoorie. The estate, situated just a little away from Mall Road, offered commanding views of the mountains, with their snow-capped peaks and thick green cover of Mansoor trees. It was lush and beautiful, but Neeraj, being blind, could not enjoy the scenery. Eventually, boredom overcame him. He decided to walk to Chic Chocolate, where he was bound to run into a friend or two. These were not his school friends but residents who often hung out at the only decent cafe in Mussoorie. The conversation would range from politics to films to cricket, and Neeraj enjoyed spending many an evening there.

Neeraj would buy a cup of coffee and settle himself at a table where he could listen to the discussions and also participate in them. Thanks to being able to access information on Braille, he was aware of all that was going on in the country. That cold November evening, the topic of discussion in the cafe was the assassination of Prime Minister Indira Gandhi. The incident occurred only a few days ago on 31 October 1984. The news had saddened Neeraj.

When the clock struck eight, Neeraj was jolted out of his thoughts. He had invited a bunch of neighbourhood friends to his house at night, and there he was, oblivious of the time. He got up in a hurry and said, 'Oh, they would be waiting for me.' Amarjit offered to drop him home but Neeraj declined. He did not want anyone to help him out of a sense of pity, and besides, he had enough experience to cover half a kilometre on his own. If he walked downhill from Mall Road, crossed Green Restaurant, turned left from the Tavern, and crossed the bridge—he would be home.

Neeraj climbed the last three steps leading up to his front door and took out the keys. He fumbled a bit till he found the keyhole. But the door was not locked. As he stepped inside the house, he sensed that someone was present. 'Are my friends here?' he asked but got no reply. He asked again, 'I know you are there. Aren't you? Stop playing with me. I can feel your presence. Remember, I have a strong sense of hearing.'

Neeraj was fond of his friends. They lived nearby and would drop in whenever they wanted, irrespective of time. It had become a sort of routine for them to come over at the end of the day and spend some time together. He enjoyed the camaraderie and the laughter. He felt alone when they left, trapped in his solitary confinement.

'Yes, we are here, Neeraj,' came a female voice. 'We've been waiting. Raghu Kaka made us coffee. While you were enjoying yourself at Chic Chocolate, we were enjoying his delicious coffee here.'

It was Meenal, a close friend and a tenant at his estate. She asked chirpily, 'So what happened at the bakery? What was the topic of discussion? Anything interesting, or was it the usual film discussions among your film buffs?'

'The discussion today was rather depressing,' he replied.

'Same old stories about how Doon Valley and Mussoorie were developed?'

Raj spoke now, 'No jokes, huh? Only boring historical stuff then?'

'At first, Negi told a joke but later the subject turned dark. He talked about how some of his friends had told him about the assassination of the prime minister,' replied Neeraj, keeping his stick aside.

Shantanu spoke next. 'These days, all we hear about is death. There's no respite from it. Can't you share a joke you heard at the cafe so that we can laugh away our gloom?'

Neeraj said, 'Yes, let's not discuss such things; let's enjoy the cool breeze and have fun.'

Neeraj recalled a joke he had recently heard: 'A doctor doing surgery on a patient lying on the operating table says, "Don't worry Vinod, everything will be all right. Nothing will go wrong. The operation will be a success." The patient lying on the table feels reassured and says, "That's great, Doctor Sahib, but my name is not Vinod." The doctor replies, "Yes, yes, I know you are Din Dayal. Vinod is my name."'

All five friends—Shantanu, Raj, Meenal, Bindu and Balvinder—burst out laughing. Meenal, the most vivacious of the lot, continued to laugh even when the others had stopped. 'Oh Neeraj, you're so funny,' she said, 'I wish we could spend more time with you. But alas, we've got responsibilities now and don't have the free time we had as children.' Neeraj nodded wistfully, 'Yes. We've grown up. We need to learn to stand on our own two feet. See, I am fifteen years old. How I wish I could see my image in the mirror.'

Neeraj was aware that all his friends lived with their parents in the outhouses, Shanker Cottages as they were known, while he, their rich landlord, lived in the main building. The banter took on a sombre tone when they discussed events that took place two years ago. 'Oh yes,' said Balvinder, 'in that accident, all of us almost died. Thank God, we were saved and are sitting with you and enjoying hot coffee at your expense.' This lightened the atmosphere, making everyone laugh.

The conversation carried on for a while till Neeraj finally said, 'I'm tired now and a little hurt too. Let's call it a day. We shall meet again tomorrow.'

'Okay, but please, we want to hear you play the piano before we leave,' said Bindu. The others joined in the chorus, 'Please play. Please play for us.' Bindu kneeled before him, folding her hands in appeal, not that he could see her, and said, 'You know how much love I have for music. I could listen to your Beethoven rendition for hours, especially his Eroica and the Fifth Symphony.'

Neeraj smiled, got up, and counted five steps, then turned and counted the eight remaining steps that brought him to the piano in his large drawing room. He sat down and began playing their favourite tunes. His friends applauded warmly after each symphony that he played effortlessly. Finally exhausted, Neeraj said, 'Okay, guys, goodnight now. And goodbye.'

After bidding them goodbye, he shut the main door, came towards his room, moved six steps to the right to reach his almirah, and felt inside for his woollen pyjamas. He changed into his night suit after neatly folding his day clothes and placing them on a shelf. He got into bed and realized he was still wearing his dark glasses. He took them off and gently placed them on the side table. Within minutes, he fell into a deep slumber—a gentle snore being the only sound breaking the silence. Even in his dreams, he could not visualize anything specific. He knew many items by touch but he had no idea of their shape or colour or design. All was blank when he was awake. And so, too, were his dreams.

The rain continued its steady percussion through the night, turning from a drizzle to a downpour by morning. The sound of the wind lashing against the windowpanes awoke Neeraj. He pulled his blanket around him. He liked the rainy weather. Being all tucked up inside gave him a cosy feeling. But a window had accidentally remained open. It was banging against the grille and he got up to shut it. As he fastened it shut, he heard a knock on the door. Some intuition told him it may be Asha. Could it be Asha? The possibility sent a little shiver of anticipation down his spine. Some years ago, he would be annoyed at the way she walked in and out of his house anytime she liked, chattering away. It felt like an intrusion. But recently, a different emotion had begun to stir in him. He wanted to be near her, to be physically closer. He wanted to touch her. He felt a sensation of desire he hadn't felt before. It was awkward. He asked his classmates in school why he felt this only towards a girl, not a boy. He wanted to know if there was any difference between a boy and a girl. He received only vague answers.

He measured the ten steps from his bedroom and entered his drawing room. Another eleven steps and he opened the door. It was indeed Asha, standing and giggling at the door. A special fragrance seemed to emanate from her, like a garden in full bloom. Maybe she was wearing an imported perfume, he thought. He shivered a little on sensing that she was close by.

She asked, 'How are you, Neeraj?' She then started to say something and stopped. 'Oh, you've hurt yourself again. Did you slip in the bathroom?'

'No, no. It's just a minor bruise,' he replied with a shrug. 'I tripped on a stone last night while walking downhill towards the house. I'm used to such mishaps. It's nothing. I reckon it would be just a bruise on my forehead and my knees.'

'Still, let me put some ointment on it. It will heal quickly,' she said and picked up his first-aid kit, took out the bottle of Dettol, poured some on the cotton wool, and pressed it against his forehead. 'Does it hurt?' she asked.

'No. Not at all. These small injuries don't hurt. It only hurts when people laugh at me. Last evening at Chic Chocolate, I could not keep the cup properly on the table, and it fell and broke. Many people laughed. To me, it wasn't funny at all,' he said sadly.

Asha removed the Band-Aid from the wrapper and placed it neatly on the wound. Her closeness sent a thrill down Neeraj's spine. She then asked him to fold up his pyjamas so that she could affix a Band-Aid on his knees too.

'Why are you smiling, Neeraj? What happened?' she asked mischievously.

'Nothing. I just had a strange feeling when you touched me, Asha.'

She giggled and moved closer. 'Like what, Neeraj?' she asked, running a finger over his face. 'What kind of strange things? Tell me.'

'Oh no, personal stuff. Things better not discussed with the opposite sex,' he laughed.

Asha lowered her voice and whispered in his ear, 'Maybe I can help you understand these strange things.' She took his hand in hers. He could barely control himself when she touched his forehead and knees. But holding a hand was just too much for the fifteen-year-old.

Just then, Raghu Kaka, Neeraj's caretaker, entered the house. Neeraj felt like caressing her, but Asha quickly let go of his quivering hand and ran out of the house. Raghu had seen her holding his hand but ignored it. Asha was three years older than Neeraj, and in those hilly areas, was certainly perceived as a woman of marriageable age.

Raghu came every day to take care of Neeraj's daily chores—washing his clothes, cooking his meals, and tending to any other needs he may have. Neeraj's father paid him well and also gave him a regular sum to buy toiletries, fruits and vegetables for his son. Raghu often inflated the prices of the items he bought, something Neeraj's father was well aware of but chose to ignore. There was no alternative to Raghu. If Raghu was making some money on the side, so be it. His son was blind and not many servants were available in Mussoorie to look after Neeraj and his estate. Most had left the hill station for greener pastures.

While Raghu was doing his daily rounds, Neeraj's aunt from Vikas Hut came bustling in. She enquired about Neeraj's health and asked if he needed anything. After hearing that he was fine and needed nothing, she left. Once a week, she reported his well-being to his father via a trunk call that she made from the Mussoorie post office situated near Kwality Restaurant.

Raghu had finished his chores and was getting ready to leave. He seemed to be in a hurry. 'I won't be coming tomorrow,' he announced. 'I've cleaned the house and washed your clothes. I've made the food for your lunch and dinner tomorrow as well. I must leave now because I have to catch the bus to attend my nephew's wedding in Dehradun. I will be gone for two days. Will you be able to manage all by yourself, Neeru Baba?'

'It's okay, Raghu Kaka, I'll manage,' Neeraj said with confidence.

Soon after that, Raghu left. It started to rain again. Neeraj bolted the door and sat down with his Braille system. He had barely spent ten minutes when there was a knock on the door again. Could Asha have come back? It was Amarjit Singh. 'Hi Brother, I heard you were hurt yesterday. Are you okay?' he asked. 'Yes, Buddy, I'm absolutely fine, thanks for your concern,' Neeraj replied in a single breath.

Amarjit persuaded Neeraj to come with him. Neeraj, however, was not inclined. He said the rain was likely to get heavier. 'But, Boss, before you leave, tell me something,' Neeraj said. 'Why do I feel so strange when Asha touches me? This morning, all she did was put a Band-Aid on my wound, and it felt like a 440-volt current ran through me. Why don't I feel this when you touch me? Is something abnormal happening to me?'

Amarjit laughed. 'Stupid, it is because you are a normal boy that you have this feeling. It's the feeling of attraction for a girl.'

'Ah, so touching a female is different from touching a male?' Neeraj asked with genuine curiosity.

'She's a woman. In this area, eighteen-year-olds are ripe enough for marriage. She has a different appeal to you and exists in your imagination differently than I do. It's natural for you to feel different if she touches you than if I do. That's just the way it is, my friend.' Amarjit said candidly.

'I wonder how she looks. I've been told by Raghu that she is fair and has long hair and big eyes. And, that she's a couple of inches shorter than me but rather voluptuous. What does that mean?'

'How would I know?' Amarjit laughed. 'Doesn't your Braille system have an answer to that?' he asked with a mischievous smile. 'Well, to tell you the truth, she indeed is very good-looking, has sharp features and is charming.'

'Why hasn't God given me eyesight? Why can't I do what everyone else can? I want to see how she looks,' Neeraj vented his feelings.

'Look, let's go spend some time at the cafe. I would love to have coffee with some cookies while going over all this,' suggested Amarjit.

'Amar, can you take me to the cinema hall? I hear there is a good movie being screened. The name of the movie is *Hero* starring a newcomer, Jackie Shroff,' he requested Amar.

Amar replied, 'Let's go, but you will only be able to hear the dialogues. Never mind Neeraj.'

After the movie, Neeraj wanted to keep talking about Asha. He wanted to know more about the mysterious desire she seemed to arouse in him. But Amarjit's answers were vague and did not quench his curiosity. He would have to wait for nature to provide those answers.

Amarjit dropped him off at the estate. Neeraj went inside and ate the dinner Raghu had left for him on the dining table. After this, he resumed his work on the Braille system. Suddenly, it started raining heavily. The weather outside grew rougher and strong winds began to shake the windows. Soon after, thunder and lightning added to the eerie sounds around him. The weather reflected his restless mood. He thought of going to bed early. However, he found himself getting ready to bathe after an hour. He subconsciously counted the steps to the bathroom, switched on the geyser, and arranged his towel and warm clothes neatly on a stool. He took off his clothes and stepped into the bathing area. He began to shower before getting into the bathtub. The water felt warm and comforting on his body. While he was luxuriating in the hot bath, he felt someone's gaze on him. It made him think that there was someone else in the bathroom.

According to what Neeraj knew, Raghu was away for two days. Therefore, it couldn't be him. It could either be his aunt or a burglar who was in the house at that time of the night. While he stood there contemplating, feeling both scared and curious, Neeraj suddenly detected a familiar fragrance in the air. 'Perhaps,' he thought to himself, before speaking out loud. 'Asha, is that you?'

After a minute or two had passed without any reply, Neeraj began to ask the same thing over and over again. He asked quickly and continuously, almost as if he needed to confirm that he wasn't going insane with thoughts about one particular woman. He felt that maybe he was being a little too creepy by having delusions and hallucinations over her body fragrance. As he restlessly waited for a response, a soft whisper accompanied by a heavy breath reached his left ear, while small, mushy palms tickled and sent chills down his shoulders. 'You don't have to ask clumsily and hurriedly when your senses have already given you an answer,' Asha said. 'Yes, Neeraj, it is me.'

Neeraj was embarrassed beyond belief and was at a loss for words. He tried to cover himself weakly and requested, 'Asha, please leave. Why would you barge into the bathroom when someone from the opposite sex is buck-naked inside? This is very awkward, and what if my aunt walks in? Please go out.' He pleaded with Asha, throwing his hands up in the air as if trying to catch her and push her out. However, his frantic gestures and pleading only resulted in Asha's laughter. After letting out a hearty laugh, Asha moved towards him and touched his chest with heavy breaths, caressing it to feel his muscles and skin. She then took the soap from his hand and began to rub it on his chest and shoulders. As Asha explored Neeraj's body with her touches, he felt nothing but tickles, chills running up his spine, and a rising body temperature, enhanced by the sensation of her heavy breath on his skin. He was getting turned on, but he was too flustered to fully comprehend it. Although Neeraj protested, his voice was so weak that he could barely hear himself. He stood still while she worked on him, rubbing soap on his arm, back and legs. He was excited by the prospect of being touched by a girl, especially without knowing where she would touch next. His heart rate began to increase; his body and mind were experiencing new emotions and thoughts that he had never encountered before. Soon, his body, following those thoughts and feelings, gave in to his instincts.

As Neeraj became aroused, Asha did not shy away from expressing more physical intimacy. She leaned in closer, to the point where her breasts and his chest were pressed together, sliding against each other due to the soap. She was intentionally trying to make him feel her bare skin and body warmth. She then took his hand and placed the soap in it, guiding his hand to touch her body. Feeling the curves of her body was thrilling, and Neeraj's hands moved on their own as if he had control over her body. Asha's soft, smooth skin made him want to do more than just rub soap onto her body. His hands began to take their own detours over her body. He moved closer to her as she gasped slightly with pleasure.

As they were showering together and washing the soap off, they couldn't resist it anymore. They finally held each other and kissed, and even the cold shower felt steamy. The water droplets on their bodies slid against each other—some from the shower and others from their own sweat—as their skin touched and rubbed against one another's.

As their legs trembled with ecstasy, Asha took Neeraj's hand and led him out of the bath and into his bedroom. Asha pinned Neeraj down on the bed, straddled him, and guided him on where and how to touch her. He couldn't see, but that didn't keep him from learning how to give her pleasure. Although the November weather was chilly, he didn't feel cold at all. Her embrace had given him all the warmth he needed. They made love for nearly an hour. Neeraj thought to himself that for the first time, he held a girl; that for the first time, a girl approached him this way; that for the first time, he kissed, touched and felt another being like this.

When Asha got up to leave, Neeraj stopped her. 'Can't you stay a little longer?' he pleaded. She replied, 'I must go now or my grandmother will get suspicious. So far, she's been completely fine with my coming here, even encouraging me to see how you're doing. If she gets suspicious, she won't let me enter your house. You may be our landlord but in my heart of hearts, I have always wanted you. Let me go now.'

The heavenly experience of the last hour lingered on every part of Neeraj's body and mind. 'I love you so much,' he said, holding her in his arms a little longer. 'I want to be with you all the time. Though I am not able to see you, I know that you are the most beautiful girl in the world.'

'You have felt me all over,' she laughed. 'That is more than seeing me, Neeraj.'

A wave of self-pity swept over Neeraj. He once again lamented that he did not have eyesight and could not see her. 'Why me, of all the people in the world? I feel so sad that I can't see someone I love so dearly. I've never yearned for eyesight as I do now,' he uttered, cursing himself and his blindness.

'Neeraj, never say that again,' Asha said firmly. 'The biggest obstacle to happiness is undervaluing what we have and overvaluing what others have. <u>Become a flower that gives fragrance even to the hand that crushes it.</u>' Her words sank deep into him and had a lasting effect. She continued, 'When Arthur Ashe, the tennis player, was writhing in pain because of a dreaded disease, someone asked him if he felt sorry for himself, if he ever complained to God, "Why me?" Do you know what he said? He said that when out of millions of tennis aspirants, he was selected to be one of the fifty players to play in Wimbledon, he didn't ask God, "Why me?" When he won the finals and was holding the coveted trophy, he didn't ask, "Why me?" If he didn't ask that question when good things came his way, why should he do so when faced with a challenge?

'Neeraj, never ask this question. All of us have difficult issues to deal with. A wise person plays with the hand he's been dealt with. And look at your blessings, you have a doting father who cares for you. I don't even have a father. My grandmother is always cursing my hard-working mother, who runs a shop all by herself and bears the household expenses. We belong to the so-called "have-nots" while you belong to a category of extremely rich people. So never complain or ask "Why me?"'

'You are probably right, but you are missing an important aspect of my life. I have grown up without a mother. My mother died the day I was born, and that's why my father has never celebrated my birthday,' said Neeraj.

'That may be true, Mr Neeraj Kapoor, but you only realize the value of a father's protective hand on your head when you don't have one.' Asha suddenly changed the topic. 'Hey, tell me why your maternal grandfather kept your mother's name Yasho Tejaswini Kumari Mehrotra. And after marriage too, when she could have shortened her name, she decided to go with Yasho Tejaswini Kumari Kapoor. It's such a unique and long name. I have always wondered why and who would keep such names in this era. Gone are the old days. Do you have any idea?' she asked.

'I don't know,' Neeraj replied. 'I didn't get the opportunity to ask her or my grandfather, but I know that my father always called her Yashiji. Yes, I do understand that Yasho Tejaswini is a unique name and one of a kind. Even in those days, the trend was to keep names such as Lata, Pushpa, and not Yasho Tejaswini.'

Asha changed the topic again. 'Listen, Neeraj, I know a lot has been missing in your life, but there are people who have faced adversity after adversity with no support. What happens to us isn't as important as our response to it. Joy and sadness keep coming and going like the breeze. So, why worry? And tell me, didn't what happened today make you happy?' Saying this with a smile, Asha opened the door and ran towards her home. The tenant had given her landlord the best time of his life.

She left Neeraj in a reflective mood. Asha's words went deep into Neeraj's heart. Never again, he decided, would he take refuge in self-pity. He would forge his destiny. He would play with the hand that life had dealt him. Blindness or no blindness, he would make a mark in the world. He decided never to give in or repent. Cheerful and happy at all times, Asha was the embodiment of vitality, beauty and goodness. He exclaimed, 'Asha, why can't you stay with me forever? You do not know how much I love you.'

In the distance, Neeraj could hear Asha's grandmother scolding her. 'Where have you been, you silly girl? I was looking for you everywhere.' It had started to rain again. He settled down with a cup of tea. Neeraj had had two epiphanies in a single day. He understood for the first time the changes in his body and its hidden sources of pleasure. He also realized that life has both highs and lows and requires us to make adjustments and compromises. Our attitude towards life, whether negative or positive, has the power to lead us down completely different paths. Yes, Asha had taught him a lot that day, both by what she had said and by the spirit with which she chose to live her life.

He felt grateful. 'I feel so content and happy,' he said to himself. 'I will never again talk about how life has dealt me an unfair hand by making me blind. I will never again say, 'Why me?' He remembered a poem titled, 'Live Every Moment'. He loudly recited, 'Carry no grudges and follow the rule, be content and maintain your cool, treasure the memories in your spool.'

He fell asleep while thinking about Asha. In the morning, he was all smiles when he opened a window and called out to his neighbourhood friends. 'Hey, come over,' he yelled. Balvinder said he would join him soon and also call the others. Soon, all his friends were sitting in Neeraj's living room. He loved that his friends lived so close by that they could call out and hear each other from their homes, and could get together in a few minutes. It was so comforting to have some company. Without them, his large, empty home would have amplified his sense of loneliness.

'Where is Raghu?' Shantanu asked. 'Who will make coffee for us?'

'Raghu is on leave for two days,' Neeraj said. 'What if Bindu makes the coffee? I want to celebrate today because my life seems to have changed. I will never wallow in self-pity again. I will never brood about being blind. I am feeling very content with what I have. God has a plan for our happiness, and it arrives at the right time in our lives. Yesterday was the day for me. I am so happy; I feel life can't get any better than this.'

They all looked at him curiously, wondering what had happened to Neeraj.

'My dear friends,' he confessed, smiling shyly. 'Asha and I have developed a new relationship. Although I know that Asha will never be able to marry me, I hope to enjoy this beautiful relationship without having unrealistic expectations for the future.

Asha is good for me. I often forget the things I should remember, and remember the things I should forget. Her wisdom has given me a new perspective on life. As she once told me, "All birds find shelter when it's pouring heavily, but the eagle avoids the rain by flying above the clouds." Problems are there, but your attitude towards them makes all the difference.'

They all leaned towards him, fully attentive to every word. He continued, 'I realize how precious you all are and how lucky I am to have you. Asha taught me today that satisfaction is not always getting what you want. It's realizing how blessed you already are.'

'We are so happy for you. Now bless us as well by playing some songs on the piano,' said Meenal. The rest joined the chorus, 'Play for us, play for us.' Neeraj obliged, happily playing song after song for his friends.

When they left, Neeraj went to bed, happy and satisfied. When he woke up the next morning, it was pouring again. At noon, just as the clock struck the hour, there was a knock on the door. While an ordinary person might not have heard it amidst the heavy downpour, Neeraj's powerful sense of hearing made up for his lack of sight, allowing him to hear it loud and clear.

Even before he opened the door, he knew who it was. Asha. The fragrance announced her presence. 'Come in, Asha,' he said.

Asha smiled and said, 'I have come to say that whatever happened between us yesterday, please don't tell anyone about it. Let it stay between the two of us.'

'I'm a grown man now, Asha,' he responded. 'And I understand what you are saying. I must tell you that I have always dreamt of having you in my arms, even though I am blind. Though I have met some of my friends, I have kept that encounter, if I can call it that, to myself. I have told my friends, including Amarjit, how I feel for you—but nothing beyond that.'

'Before my grandmother comes looking for me, I must also

tell you that I have always been drawn to you. Despite your blindness, your cute face and muscular body, even at such a tender age, have sent shivers of excitement down my spine. I don't think you know how attractive you are, Neeraj.'

Neeraj was visibly annoyed. 'I am not at a "tender age" anymore. I have crossed over and will soon be turning sixteen. In Mussoorie, I can apply for a driving licence when I reach the age of sixteen. So, I am not a kid anymore.'

She smiled, moved closer, and pulled him inside the bathroom. She kissed him tenderly for almost a minute, and after spending an eventful time together, she left. This time, they both got exhausted but thoroughly enjoyed the experience.

Later in the day, around nine o'clock, Neeraj heard another knock. He opened the door and the same fragrance enveloped him. 'My family has gone to attend a marriage at Hotel Brentwood,' whispered Asha. 'They have unknowingly given us an hour to make love,' she giggled. He noticed that she had applied a liberal amount of perfume. She had made a complete surrender to him.

Neeraj couldn't believe how his life had taken a complete U-turn. The lonely existence he once knew was now a thing of the past. He had found the woman he loved, and she was in his arms. They made love for forty passionate minutes; she kept chiding him between moments of ecstasy. Neeraj was at the top of the world. He had always desired Asha, but he could never have imagined that he would be able to make love to her—that too twice in a single day. The world had suddenly turned into a colourful and exciting place.

Neeraj savoured the heady feeling of being intoxicated by Asha's love. She came over any chance she got, and their time together was spent in long, lingering embraces. They would have intimate conversations that connected them on a deeper level. Neeraj stopped calling his friends over, fearing that their visits would interrupt his time with Asha. He was the happiest he had ever been.

But all good things come to an end, sometimes sooner than expected. Five days before his vacation ended, Asha delivered the saddest news Neeraj had ever heard. She was getting married against her wishes to a rich businessman, named Raj Majheetha, from New York. Raj's parents wanted an Indian bride for their son and had advertised in the local papers. Asha's photograph was sent to them, and they immediately responded with interest. Since they had to leave for the US soon, the marriage was scheduled to take place within a few days.

Neeraj's heart sank when he heard the news. 'What do you mean you're getting married? You can't do this to me...to us. You can't leave me. I love you, Ashu. I can't live without you.'

Asha held Neeraj's hands in hers, unconcerned that her grandmother might come over searching for her. She said, 'You must reconcile yourself to the situation. I, too, had dreamed of studying science, conducting research in pharmaceuticals, or pursuing a career in electronics. But I have had to come to terms with the fact that those things won't happen for me. I agreed to this marriage because I know that I will never be able to go to the US on my own and lead a comfortable life. My fiancé is affluent and owns several petrol pumps and showrooms in the States. I have had to compromise in life. Please let me go and get married to him. Please...please...you know that my father used to run a Chinese restaurant at the library, and after he died, all the things I wanted to achieve went down the drain. Please let me go and do not make a scene,' she pleaded with folded hands.

Neeraj sat down in a daze, feeling as though the sky had fallen on him. How could this be happening? Only recently, life had granted him everything he longed for—love, pleasure, companionship—and now it was all slipping away. His beloved

Asha was begging for permission to marry another man. Soon, she would be in someone else's arms. 'I was having such a magical time with you that I even sent a message to my headmaster in Dehradun that I would return ten days later,' he said, his voice trembling. 'I have stopped calling Amarjit and my other friends over because of you. Please don't leave Asha, please don't get married.' He folded his hands, tears rolling down his cheeks. 'Please wait a couple of years, and we will get married. I will get my father and your mother to agree. Please, Asha.'

'The die is cast, Neeraj. Neither of us can do anything about it. You are too young for marriage, and I am of marriageable age. You are a rich man's son, while I belong to a poor family. We come from very different worlds. My mother has struggled a lot after my father's death, and I can't bear to disappoint her.' She stopped, letting out a sigh. 'In this world, a woman has to sacrifice a lot.'

As Asha turned to leave, she stopped and faced Neeraj once more. She spoke her last words to him in Mussoorie: 'We were not destined to be together in this life. I hope that I become your spouse in the next life.' She paused and added, 'My mother has asked my sister, Shobha, to keep in touch with you and take care of you. Neeraj, life is made up of different chapters. Our love was just one chapter, and it has come to an end.'

Neeraj refused to give up. 'Asha, my mother left this world when I was born, and you are leaving me when I have barely understood the meaning of life. Please do not go.'

Asha did not reply. She kissed him. And with that, she was gone.

❧

With Asha gone, Neeraj became a recluse and barely spoke to anyone. Amarjit came over a few times, so did Shobha, but Neeraj barely responded to them. He appeared to have lost his spirit. After Asha's marriage, he had even stopped going to Chic Chocolate and did not touch his piano. He no longer called his friends over to spend the evening with him. He withdrew into himself, rarely venturing out anymore.

Shobha began to drop in at odd hours, especially when Raghu was away, but he showed no interest in her. Shobha had an agenda of her own. She was having an affair with Rajesh, a handsome playboy from Mussoorie. He would stealthily follow her into Neeraj's house, and quietly settle into a corner room of Neeraj's very large home. Neeraj was so lost in his thoughts that, even with his powerful sense of hearing, he failed to sense Rajesh's entry into the house. Taking advantage of Neeraj's blindness, Shobha would slip into the corner room. Neeraj would bolt the door after Shobha pretended to leave. She would, however, run into the arms of Rajesh. They had found the ideal love nest for themselves, hidden in plain sight. Neeraj had no inkling of this secret rendezvous at his own home, right under his nose.

Shobha and Rajesh often came to make love in the last of the thirteen rooms on the first floor of Shankar Estate. One evening, as the harsh winter rain continued, Neeraj was overcome by loneliness and reached out to his five friends. He wanted someone to talk to, and one by one, they came over to his house.

'How have you been?' Bindu was the first to arrive.

'I'm okay,' Neeraj replied. 'This is my last day of vacation. I have to go back to Dehradun tomorrow. Unfortunately, Raghu can't make coffee for you since he's gone to the market to buy some vegetables.' He paused and then shared something that had been disturbing him, 'Listen, Bindu, Shobha has been acting strangely for the past few days. She comes here, enquires about my well-being, behaves somewhat awkwardly, and leaves within minutes. Something feels amiss.'

Bindu giggled. 'Are you sure she's alone?'

Before he could answer, Shobha and Rajesh came into the room, a little out of breath as if they had been running. 'Neeraj, who are you talking to?' asked Shobha. 'And, why are you telling strangers things about us?' she added. Rajesh did not breathe a word.

'I'm talking to my five close friends: Meenal, Bindu, Balvinder, Shantanu and Raj. Can't you see them? They are all here in this room.'

'Neeraj, are you mad? There's no one here. We were in the other room. When we heard you talking to someone, we quickly wanted to leave your house. But there's no one here. Are you crazy?'

Neeraj raised his voice. 'Before I ask my friends to speak to you, tell me what were you doing in my house without my permission? Balvinder and Raj, please tell this guy to leave my house at once and to never come back. That goes for you too, Shobha.'

Rajesh let out a ghoulish laugh. 'Five friends?' he said. 'You're not only blind, you're crazy too. The five friends you just mentioned have been dead for two years. They died two years ago in a car accident while going to Barlowganj. They had gone for a picnic to Maussi Falls, and on their way back, they had a terrible accident with a Dehradun Roadways bus. They all died on the spot, don't you remember? All of Mussoorie knows about the tragic accident.'

Neeraj felt as if someone had punched him in the gut. 'What are you saying, Rajesh? They have come over many times. We've spent many evenings together, chatting and playing. They've even begged me to play the piano. You are mistaken. They somehow survived. They've come over every time I called them.'

Rajesh turned to Shobha. 'See, I told you he is mad. I'm getting scared of being here with him and his five ghosts at this late hour. Let's leave before the ghosts appear in front of us. Why did I ever agree to come with you to this godforsaken place?'

Shobha punched him with her elbow. 'Rajesh, shut up. Don't you realize the cat is now out of the bag?'

'Do what you want Shobha. I am not staying here for another minute.' Saying that, Rajesh ran out of the house. Shobha followed him.

When they had left, the five friends began to laugh. It did not seem to bother Neeraj that he was speaking to ghosts.

He turned to Meenal and uttered with a tinge of sadness, 'Shobha was making an utter fool of me, entering my home like a thief. They used me. Why did she do this to me?'

Meenal replied, 'We don't want to discuss Shobha and Rajesh. Gossips are worse than thieves because they steal another person's dignity, honour and reputation. We should learn how to live with a positive bent of mind. Many people have to endure massive problems, but some of them still continue to face them with a smile on their lips. Just like a flute that has several holes on its body, but the sound that emanates from it is really soothing."

Bindu added, 'Forget about them, Neeraj. Find good people and leave the bad ones alone.'

Then she paused and stated, 'Now that you have learnt that you've been talking to dead people all this while, we shall leave and never return.'

Neeraj was devastated. He needed his friends; he needed company. He was not afraid of talking to dead people. Or, wait. Was he just imagining that he had spent so many evenings with his friends? He begged them to speak, but no voice came. Only an eerie silence prevailed.

First Asha left him. Now his close childhood friends were gone too. He felt like his mind would explode. He couldn't take it anymore and lost consciousness. When he woke up, he was surrounded by his relatives. His father had driven up from Delhi to be with him, and his aunt and uncle from Dehradun were present too. So was his father's brother, Pawan Prakash Uncle. Everyone was worried about Neeraj's health. He was glad that his father was by his side; he needed his support to recover from this traumatic experience. He heard all of them enquiring about him.

He never told anyone of the experiences he had had in Mussoorie. No one ever knew about his love for Asha, how Shobha and Rajesh had used him, and the many evenings he had spent with his dead friends.

After a few days of helping him to recuperate, his father took him back to school and left him in the company of his schoolmates. Even though Asha had left him in the lurch, she had also given him the key to happiness. He remembered what she had once said: it is the road you take that decides your destiny, and not your destiny that decides the road you take. If he wanted the journey of life to be comfortable, the most important thing was to let go of the baggage of expectations and create a storehouse of knowledge.

His father left for Delhi but Pawan Prakash Uncle spent some time in Dehradun looking after Neeraj. Pawan Prakash ran a successful business in Seattle and had been on a visit to India when Neeraj was taken to hospital. He sensed that Neeraj had been having conversations with imaginary people and took him to see a psychiatrist in Dehradun. The psychiatrist asked Neeraj several questions about his dead friends. He also interrogated Raghu. Afterwards, he addressed a few questions to Neeraj. 'You said that Raghu made coffee for them, but when I spoke to him, he denied ever having made coffee for your five friends. You also claim to have asked Bindu to make coffee for all of you. Do you remember her handing you a cup? Do you remember drinking it?' Neeraj's answer was in the negative.

The psychiatrist probed further. 'Was there ever anyone else in the room when your friends were talking to you?' Again, the answer was in the negative. Finally, the psychiatrist gave his diagnosis. 'Neeraj, you've been suffering from a mental disease where a lonely person has imaginary conversations with people who don't exist. It isn't as uncommon as you may think. My father used to stay in Vrindavan near Mathura. He lived alone with only an idol of Lord Krishna for company and he would occasionally talk to the idol and even imagine that the idol was talking back to him. Single children often talk to imaginary pets and playmates. These are all attempts to handle extreme loneliness. They are illusions. Once your brain realized that your friends no longer existed in real life, they disappeared.' He gave Neeraj some medication and asked him to forget about those incidents and move on.

Pawan Prakash Uncle extended his visit to India to spend more time with Neeraj, whom he loved like his own son. He was forty-four and had never married, and it seemed unlikely that he ever would. Neeraj was the only heir of the two brothers and one day destined to take over the vast empire inherited and built by them. His uncle was much more affluent than his father.

❧

In the winter of 2021, Neeraj, now fifty-two years old, was admiring the Empire State Building, which was right opposite his office in Manhattan, New York. An unexpected snowfall that morning had covered the building in white, and now the late afternoon sun seemed to touch it with an ethereal radiance. While he was lost in thought, his CEO and old friend, Amarjit, walked in. He sounded excited. 'Nancy tells me that several reporters are lined up outside the office wanting to interview you on our latest laser gun invention,' he said. 'It's amazing! For the last four

years, you've won the coveted Zenith Prize for the invention of
the year. Four years! They want to ask you how you get these
brilliant ideas. And the best news ever is that we've crossed ten
billion dollars in our net worth this year. *Forbes* has been calling
too. They want to do an exclusive with you. We must celebrate.
Oh!' he stated forcefully.

Neeraj smiled. Now tall and lean, he was the owner and
chairman of numerous companies, including New Inventions
Inc., Network Videos, Qutub Minar Inc. and India Electronics
LLC. 'As these snowflakes continue to fall, our companies' shares
continue to rise,' he said philosophically, looking out the window.
'Neeraj, we can encash some of our shares and make a fortune,'
Amarjit said, revelling in the heady feeling of success. 'Should I
try and dispose of some shares today?'

'No, not yet,' replied Neeraj. 'And I'm not going to give any
interviews or attend any business meetings today either. I am
leaving on my private plane for Washington, DC, to meet an
old friend from India, Yashwant Kainth. He works with USAID
(United States Agency for International Development) and is a
true friend. Amar, true friendship is the rarest thing in the world.
Most relationships are conditional and transactional. Only true
friendship is unconditional. Although I could take advantage
of Yashwant by promoting our products to USAID, it has never
been my intention. Yashwant isn't overawed by my success, and
our relationship is simply built on the camaraderie we have as
old friends. We don't have any hidden agenda or motive behind
our friendship. The best relationship is when both parties have a
strong desire to meet and spend quality time together. It can only
survive through mutual understanding, trust, sincerity and honesty.
Since Yashwant is here for only a couple of days, I must see him.'

Neeraj called his secretary into his plush room and asked
her to cancel all his appointments of the day with due apologies.

Amarjit did not quite agree with Neeraj's way of thinking. 'In America, a business magnate can't remain on top for long if he listens to his heart more than his head,' he said. Realizing that this would have no impact on Neeraj, he changed the subject abruptly. 'Hey, I also want to go to Washington, DC to meet my sister. She stays at Burke, and I couldn't even make it for Raksha Bandhan. She's mad at me. Can I come along with you? It might pacify her.'

Neeraj hesitated. 'Whenever you've wanted to accompany me, something or the other has come up, and I've had to cancel my appointments. But anyway, come along. We leave in the next half hour. Will that be fine?'

'Sure,' Amarjit replied. 'I just need to tell Stanley that I won't be part of the panel interviewing the new candidates today. If you don't mind, we can go to the fortieth floor, inform him and then leave directly for the airport. Washington, DC, here we come!' He raised his arms in a childlike manner as if the capital was just round the corner.

They went together to the conference room where the interviews were being held on the fortieth floor of the building. A girl who looked Indian was being interviewed by a panel of four executives from New Inventions Inc. They all got up to wish Neeraj the moment he entered. The girl was too nervous to notice what was happening. She kept sitting. Stanley signalled to her to stand up, and she did so reluctantly, with her back to the chairman of the company. After exchanging pleasantries, Neeraj told the panel in his inimitable style, a mix of formality and familiarity, that he was whisking the CEO away for a day. 'Will that be okay?' he asked. 'Sure,' said Stanley.

Neeraj looked at the girl and said in a low voice to Stanley, 'I'm always glad to see young people of Indian origin wanting to work here. I like to give them a chance. Remember, we give preference to Indians and then to others. It may not be legally correct, but one must consider those who come from one's native land. I have spent a considerable part of my life in India.'

Stanley replied, 'Yes, Sir, but we often have great difficulty pronouncing their names. Now, take this girl who has come for an interview. Her name is a real tongue-twister. Let me try… Yasho… aa… Tejjaashwane… kkkhummari, or something like that.'

Neeraj smiled, 'Let me help you. It's simply Yasho Tejaswini Kumari.' He turned to leave, but then stopped short. Who on earth would have kept a name like that, and of all places, in New York? He turned back and came forward to have a look at the girl. She was standing nervously, holding a file with her résumé and other documents. He was shocked. This girl was a replica of Asha. She had the same nose, same complexion and same black hair. She was only a little taller. Trying to control his emotions, he said, 'Mind if I interview her?' 'Sure, Sir, why not?' replied the HR manager, who was perplexed by Neeraj's sudden interest in a mere job interview. Amarjit, too, was confused. However, one look at the young candidate made him understand Neeraj's strange behaviour.

Neeraj couldn't contain the surge of emotions as he asked the girl, 'How long have you been in the US? What are your parents' names?' He was full of energy, and his demeanour unsettled the girl.

She cleared her throat and said, 'Sir, I've seen your photographs in the papers and watched your interviews on TV. You are the inventor of space shuttles as well as the OrCam V device that allows even the visually impaired to see. I am a big fan of your work. And I notice that you are wearing your invention, which is a testament to its success.'

'Yes, I am wearing one of my own inventions, which is why, despite being born blind, I can see now. But that doesn't answer my question.'

The girl replied, 'My father left us several years ago. I live with my mother in an apartment in Flushing.'

'Okay,' he replied, trying to digest this information. 'Where have you worked before or are you still employed somewhere?'

'Sir, I was with Buster Videos for almost seven years. They have recently filed a Chapter Eleven petition for bankruptcy. It's hard to believe that there was a time when video rental stores like Buster were making millions. Now they have nowhere to go. I have yet to receive my salary for the last six months. I've been unable to pay my EMIs; the future at Buster seems bleak.'

He observed that she had confidence as well as the ability to express herself honestly and fearlessly.

Neeraj exchanged a look with Amarjit and said triumphantly, 'Several years ago, in 2005, our company proposed to Buster that we could help them digitize and create an online platform for sales. Physical videos and DVDs were on their way out. The world was changing, but they didn't see it. Do you know what their directors said about our proposal? They laughed at us and said they knew the business better than anyone else. Telling them what to do was like selling ice to an Eskimo. We've outplayed them in every area. Our business models have succeeded, while they are filing for bankruptcy.'

The panel looked at Neeraj curiously. Why was he taking so much interest in a girl with so little experience? Only Amarjit understood the reasons behind Neeraj's lengthy conversation with someone he would otherwise have not even met, given that he had 32,000 employees worldwide.

Neeraj again enquired about her parents, but she said that the question was personal and irrelevant to the job she was applying for. Neeraj admired her straightforwardness and said, 'Okay, we are hiring you. You will be paid three hundred thousand dollars a year. Leave your résumé and references with our HR head. If you don't mind, Yashi, I can give you a lift home, and on the way, I can ask you more questions about your experience.'

Though she was taken aback by his behaviour, she had no option but to meekly accept his offer. The panel was dumbfounded by the brevity of the interview, the quick selection process and the remarkable salary offered. Neeraj gestured to Stanley to complete the paperwork the next day. Stanley nodded passively, confused by the turn of events. Neeraj ushered Yasho Tejaswini Kumari out of the main entrance. An eight-door limousine appeared. Michael, the chauffeur, stepped out and saluted them while holding the door open. Her confusion increased with every passing moment. She was perplexed by everything that was happening so fast. She couldn't understand why the chairman winked and gave a thumbs up to the CEO as they got into the car. She shrugged it off and thought to herself that if a big man like him wanted to visit her tiny apartment in Flushing, so be it.

She sank into the plush seats of the most luxurious car she had ever seen. 'I can't believe my luck, Sir,' she said. 'Even the US president's secretary doesn't get paid as much as you have offered me.' She paused and then asked him, 'Sir, why were you calling me Yashi?' Neeraj was enjoying talking to her. 'Coincidentally, Yasho Tejaswini was also my mother's name,' he said. 'My father used to call her Yashi. Do you know why you have such a unique name?'

She shrugged. She had no idea. Neeraj decided to open up to her. The moment had come. 'I'll tell you why you have such an unusual name. Because a long time ago, your mother used to be my tenant and neighbour in Mussoorie. Because we used to meet almost daily. Because she understood a blind boy's needs. Because she knew Yasho Tejaswini was my mother's name. Because she inspired me to become what I have become today, despite my disability. Because I was always in love with her."

He paused. Yashi looked at him, completely stunned. Neeraj

continued, 'Of course you wouldn't know any of this. I'm baffled that your mother never called me even though we've been living in the same city for a while now. She must have read about me; there's been a lot of coverage. We were so close once. Why did she never call me?'

Yashi replied, 'Maybe she wanted to hide our circumstances and our poverty from you. My mother had a very difficult time from the day she got married. She was told that my father was a rich businessman in the US. But after marriage, she discovered that he worked as a bus conductor and a part-time driver. Nor was he living in Long Island as he had told my grandmother. He stayed in one of the poorest neighbourhoods in the city. She had been duped. Whenever she protested, he would beat her up. He was often violent with her. She had nowhere to go. Imagine the plight of an eighteen-year-old bride far from home: her in-laws have snatched her passport; she is sometimes locked up in the storeroom; she has no one to turn to; and she discovers that she is pregnant. Those were my mother's circumstances. She had no choice but to accept her fate.

'But the deception didn't end there. There was another shock waiting for her. She discovered that her husband was already married. He had married an American woman for immigration purposes and was still in touch with her. It took my mother six long years to escape from his clutches. After she had found a job at a drug store and we had moved into our current flat, she sued him. That is where we are headed—our one-room flat in Flushing.'

Neeraj felt his heart fill with tenderness and protectiveness for the woman he had loved all these years. What a difficult time she had had. He felt a surge of anger towards her duplicitous ex-husband. How dare he put his hands on his beloved? By the time they reached Flushing, Neeraj was overcome by emotion. His heart was pounding as they stepped into the lift. Yashi pressed the button for the fourth floor.

Asha opened the door. She was fifty-five years old but looked much older. Her hardships had left an imprint on her. The moment she saw Neeraj with her daughter, she knew that he had unearthed the truth about her past.

They looked at each other for a long moment, neither moving nor saying anything. Yashi broke the silence, 'Mom, can we come in?'

A tear rolled down Asha's cheek. 'I had asked her not to go for an interview at your company,' she said, her voice trembling. 'But I couldn't convince her…'

He stopped her. 'Why Asha? Why should you stop her? Why? If you didn't want to meet me, then why give her the name Yasho Tejaswini? You knew that, somewhere, you wanted to stay connected with me.'

'Perhaps, you're right,' she replied with a lump in her throat. 'I saw your interview and how proudly you spoke about your invention OrCam V. No longer timid and unsure of yourself, you have become a different person from who you were at Shanker Estate.'

'Yes, mother, you're right,' Yashi piped in. 'OrCam V has helped so many visually impaired people across the world in not just seeing but also achieving self-reliance. It has single-handedly changed so many people's destinies.'

'Yes, not only is it effective and easily wearable, but it also has many other features to help blind people enjoy the beauty of the world,' he said. He turned and looked at Asha directly, 'I am looking at you for the first time in person, and that's a miracle for me. You were the inspiration for this invention. Your face was the first one I wanted to see. I wanted to see what the girl I have loved all my life looked like. I had no idea where you had disappeared, Asha. Once I could see, I tried to find you on Facebook and Instagram, but to no avail. I finally sent my assistant to Mussoorie International School to get your photograph. It was with great difficulty that he managed to find one and mail it to me. That was the time I first used my invention. The first person I wanted to see was you, no one else. And in that photograph, I saw the most beautiful woman in the world, just as you still are.'

'Ah, I am old now, Neeraj. The lines on my face tell a sad tale,' she replied.

'No, Ashu, beauty lies in the eyes of the beholder. To me, there is no woman more beautiful than you. The time we were in love with each other was truly precious. I would have given my right arm just to be with you. Now I am going to do what I should have done then but could not because I was blind and too young.' He got down on his knees and asked, 'Asha, will you please marry me?'

She blushed as she walked gently into his arms. 'Do you know why I tolerated my ex-husband's abuse and why I named my daughter after your mother?' she said, overcome with emotion. 'The truth is that Yashi is your daughter. I found that I was already pregnant when I landed in New York. I have kept it a secret all these years. Even my daughter doesn't know that you are her real father.'

The billionaire chairman of New Inventions Inc. absorbed this information in complete silence. He was stunned. How much had changed in a single day? He walked across to Yashi, who was dumbfounded by what her mother had just revealed. He embraced his daughter with tears in his eyes. He said, 'Start packing my child, we are all going to stay together at my mansion in Long Island.' He turned to Asha and told her, 'Your first husband had lied to you, but I am not lying.' Not letting go of Yashi, he proclaimed, 'My dear daughter Yasho Tejaswini, granddaughter of

Yasho Tejaswini. If it hadn't been for your name, we may never have discovered each other. Today, I have my beloved back and gained a daughter as well. How much that was lost has been found today!'

All of them were overwhelmed by the change in their fortune. Neeraj broke the silence. 'Asha, if you recollect, you changed my attitude completely—you converted this docile, gullible, stupid boy into a man of substance. Your words of wisdom struck a chord with me, and I became resolutely positive in my attitude. You regenerated my fifth sense, inspiring me to shed the tag of 'blindness' and work harder than ever before.' Neeraj smiled and bowed at the idol of Lord Shiva installed at a small temple in a corner of the house. 'As a wise man once said, a thread of love and a needle of emotional support can mend broken and frayed relationships. And so, as a successful businessman, I'm willing to marry you and legally adopt Yasho Tejaswini as my daughter,' declared Neeraj.

'But Neeraj, a lot of water has flowed under the bridge. Times have changed and things have changed. Now, there is a big difference between you and me. Two banks of the same river can never meet,' lamented Asha.

'Asha, you are like quicksilver; when someone wrongs you, you glide away without retaliation. It's been some time since your deceitful husband left you. Such people are not worth worrying over—they are as full of lies as a faulty sieve.' He paused for a moment, before continuing, 'I have always spoken the truth. I think the greatest advantage of speaking the truth is that you do not have to remember what you said. The price of deceit is before you.'

Neeraj persisted, 'Do not hesitate to accept my proposal. I know you find yourself in a predicament all of a sudden. Believe me, this will be mutually beneficial. We shall give dear Yashi a remarkable future, and we will be happy together.' Asha was still unsure. She looked at her daughter, who was also perplexed.

Neeraj spoke again, 'You know what, the first person you think of in the morning and the last person you think of before going to bed is the cause of your happiness or pain. It was you who shared these pearls of wisdom when it was raining heavily in Mussoorie. You also said that all birds find shelter on a rainy day, but it's only an eagle that finds strength and avoids rain by flying over the clouds. Problems may be there but our will makes all the difference. Please say yes to my proposal, however sudden it might be,' he pleaded.

Yasho Tejaswini touched her mother's shoulder, 'Mother, please accept my...err...father's proposal. I can feel his emotions and unparalleled love for you. His words are full of sincerity.'

Asha smiled at Neeraj and said, 'I accept your proposal. I am willing to become your wife.'

FIVE

ZORAWAR SINGH – NAPOLEON OF THE EAST

In November 1841, a fifty-seven-year-old Hindu warrior stopped at the foot of Mount Kailash, considered the abode of Lord Shiva, in Tibet. He took a dip in the holy water of Lake Mansarovar and offered his prayers as a devout follower of Lord Shiva. In the pellucid water of the lake, he could see his reflection clearly. Looking back at him was a brave and ferocious warrior determined to reclaim the entire northern belt from Chinese and Tibetan rulers as well as establish peace at the borders of the Xinjiang province in China.

The warrior twirled his moustache and, being a true patriot, felt a surge of pride in his achievements. His second in command, Mehta Basti Ram, was also taking a dip in the holy water. Mehta Basti Ram found his General, Zorawar Singh, in a contemplative mood and quickly discerned what was occupying the thoughts of his chieftain. He drew nearer to his General and said, 'Some call you the "Lion of the Mountain", while our Dogra king, the mighty ruler of Jammu and Kashmir, has bestowed the title of "Napoleon of the East" on you. The world recognizes that our triumph over the Chinese in the Xinjiang province was made possible by your indomitable courage and great strategies. You have fought and won many battles, expanding the Dogra Empire from the Galwan Valley in Ladakh to Tibet and China and from the Wakhan corridor of Afghanistan to the Khyber Pakhtunkhwa province. You are known for your valour throughout India, and many soldiers wish to emulate you.'

The General looked back at Mehta Basti Ram and spoke with all humility, 'If it is God's will for us to expand our empire from east to west, then it shall come to pass. Long live our king, Maharaja Gulab Singh. We have defeated the Tibetans and their Chinese allies and captured the strategic fort of Chi-T'ang. We have vanquished our enemies and consolidated the Dogra Empire—from northern Tibet to Punjab, and from the eastern to western parts of Afghanistan. I have learned many strategies from none other than the great Maharaja Ranjit Singh. He was instrumental in instilling fear among the British and Mughal rulers in this part of our great country. Only Maharaja Ranjit Singh and his unyielding Sikh warriors could have defeated the Afghans and stretched the borders of India to Afghanistan.'

He continued, 'I am putting you in command of the Chi-T'ang fort. You must defend it from any Chinese attack. They may outnumber us, but they lack courage. It is not numbers that win wars; it is courage that paves the way for victory. Even a small contingent of five thousand soldiers can defeat an army of twenty thousand by showing an unconquerable spirit.' He paused, allowing Mehta Basti Ram to respond. 'General, I fully endorse your views. The Chinese came from all sides, and it is difficult for us to fight in these mountainous regions, especially due to frostbite and the lack of oxygen in these areas. Survival itself is a challenge, not to mention the formidable task of fighting the Chinese. Defeating them was next to impossible, but you accomplished that feat. No Indian General has ever been able to beat them and push them back to their territory in Xinjiang from Galwan Valley. You have not only overpowered the Chinese but also taught them a lesson. You will be remembered for this monumental achievement. Maharaja Gulab Singh is very pleased with you. The messenger who had just arrived said that the king has bestowed upon you many *jaagirs* (estates) and a fort for defeating the Tibetans and the Chinese. This reward is also for your patriotism and valour. The name of General Zorawar Singh will be written in gold in the annals of history. The only General to defeat the Chinese in the east and the Afghans in the west.'

Mehta paused for a reaction, but there was none. He continued, 'Sir, you are truly the Lion of the Mountain. When you roar, the enemy runs away. You strike like lightning and create mayhem for your opponents. You have the power of an elephant, the courage of a lion, the eyes of an eagle, and the sharp mind of a fox.'

No matter how much praise was bestowed on him, Zorawar remained humble. He took another dip and signalled for a towel and his clothes. The strong, muscular body of Zorawar Singh, the wazir of a vast empire, had many marks of injuries on his body. Thinking back, Zorawar remembered saving a princess of Kashmir. This heroic act earned him a recommendation from the King of Kashmir himself, allowing him to join the imperial knight order. The princess of Kashmir was on a visit to Bhagirathi, where Zorawar lived. Zorawar was loitering by the banks of the river when he saw the beautiful princess on horseback. It so happened that her horse, a rare Arab stallion, moved ahead of the entourage. The horse wandered too close to the river and an alligator charged out of the water towards the princess. Sensing danger, the horse ran wild and threw the princess off. The princess landed ten feet away from the ferocious alligator, which intended to grab the princess by the leg and drag her towards the river. Without hesitation, Zorawar ran to the princess's aid, engaging in a physical battle with the alligator to keep it from harming her, while shouting, 'Please take cover behind the mound while I try to tackle this monster.'

The princess was traumatized and frozen in fear, to the point where she could barely stay in her senses, let alone run away to escape from the jaws of the alligator. Noticing this, Zorawar decided to prioritize taking the princess to a safe distance and calming her nerves instead of killing the alligator. While struggling to contain the alligator, he started to look for a way to distract it, so the princess could flee from the scene. Just as Zorawar was about to lose his grip, the alligator opened its mouth to bite off his head. Zorawar saw an opportunity and quickly grabbed a nearby tree branch, shoving it into the alligator's mouth. The creature shifted its focus to removing the branch, allowing Zorawar to rush to the petrified princess, scoop her up in his arms, and carry her swiftly to safety.

Zorawar's heroic act did not go unnoticed, as attendants and officers of the entourage witnessed his bravery. News of his feat reached the King of Kashmir, who ordered his subordinates to praise Zorawar and present him with a hundred gold coins, as well as a recommendation for the imperial army. Overnight, Zorawar became not only famous but also rich. His parents were filled with pride for their brave son.

On another occasion, Zorawar's bravery shone through when he defeated a python. He and his friends ventured into the forbidden forest across the Bhagirathi River, which had always been off-limits due to its dense and unexplored nature. Despite the cautionary tales, Zorawar and his friends craved adventure and wandered into the land.

While exploring the forest, they stumbled upon a tree full of ripe fruits. Unable to resist, Zorawar climbed the tree and began picking fruit, but he was caught off guard when an Indian python suddenly coiled around him. Zorawar's friends tried to free him by throwing stones at the predator, but it was no use. The python was determined to devour its prey.

In a stroke of luck, one of Zorawar's friends hit the python's right eye with a stone, causing both the serpent and its victim to fall to the ground. With a momentary reprieve, Zorawar seized a blunt stone and struck the python in the head, causing it to lose consciousness. His friends helped him escape the python's grip, and the trio ran towards the river to cross to safety. From a young age, Zorawar had always shown a warrior's spirit and refused to back down in the face of danger.

Zorawar was not the one to cower before the enemy. Before embarking on a journey with his army of ten thousand men through the difficult terrain to the battlefield of To-Yo, the northeastern frontier of India, he bowed in humility.

Zorawar had expanded the Dogra Empire for over 724 kilometres of inhospitable terrain, constructing numerous forts and palaces from Srinagar to the Chinese borders. He was resting in the Chi-T'ang fort near Taklakot, where his army was facing intense cold, combined with rain, snowfall and lightning. Many of his soldiers had lost their fingers and toes to frostbite. He had ordered his soldiers to burn the wooden stock of their muskets to warm themselves. His scouts had informed him that the Chinese, who had been earlier defeated by him, were regrouping at To-Yo. The Chinese could strike any time along with Gyalpo, the former ruler of Ladakh, who had revolted against his king—the ruler of Jammu and Kashmir.

Zorawar Singh came out of his room into the bitter cold and walked up to the ramparts of the fort to inspect the alertness of his sentries. While walking on the ramparts, he noticed a herd of deer struggling to escape from an enormous white tiger. With the snow-covered track hampering their movement, the deer were easy prey for the tiger. It struck Zorawar that if the deer managed to escape, the tiger would change its strategy and assault his sentries stationed outside the main gate of the fort. He immediately took a lance from one of his soldiers and jumped from the wall which was ten feet high. He charged towards the tiger. On seeing Zorawar's threatening pose and stance, the tiger stopped its pursuit of the deer and shifted its focus to attack the General instead. Zorawar was ready for the tiger's charge. The animal lunged at him. Zorawar ducked in the nick of time, and the tiger fell on the snow-laden mountain path. Zorawar realized that the tiger's claws had ruptured his skin. Although the tiger inflicted a minor injury, it was not enough to dissuade Zorawar from killing the beast or sending a message that it would be wise to go back to the Chinese territory from which it came.

He heard a voice from behind. Mehta was rushing to his aid with soldiers wielding muskets and swords. Zorawar signalled for them to stop. As the ferocious predator prepared to engage in combat with the formidable warrior, the commander and soldiers stood motionless.

The tiger realized that it was a do-or-die situation for him and got into an attacking position. The cunning predator climbed a rock to gain a strategic advantage before pouncing on the warrior. Anticipating the tiger's move, Zorawar raised his lance upwards, and as the tiger launched itself at him, he swiftly got out of the way. He was agile enough to dodge the tiger once again. Although he had fallen, Zorawar kept his lance pointed directly at the tiger. As their eyes met, the brave warrior signalled for the predator to withdraw.

Zorawar shouted, 'The hunter has suddenly become the hunted and is sure to lose his life. I will use your skin to cover myself and hang your head on the wall of the Chi-T'ang fort. Either you run back to your Chinese territory or get killed.' Surprisingly, the tiger seemed to sense the looming threat and quickly retreated towards the Chinese border, vanishing from sight. The tiger had been injured by the lance wielded by Zorawar.

Mehta saw blood oozing out of the General's lower abdomen after he had single-handedly confronted the tiger in such frigid conditions. He asked Ram Karan, the hakim, to attend to his master immediately as the bleeding needed to be stemmed. He also noticed that the Chinese patrol stationed at the Xinjiang border had observed Zorawar Singh's valour, which caused their shoulders to sag further in dejection. Zorawar had indirectly conveyed to the Chinese to keep their distance or face the same fate as the tiger.

Zorawar was lying in his room while the hakim attended to him. The hakim carefully applied a medicinal paste and wrapped a bandage around Zorawar's wounded abdomen. Luckily, for Zorawar, the bleeding had been stemmed. The claws of the dreaded animal had caused only a surface-level injury. The hakim spoke at last, 'This is not an age to be so adventurous. You have had a very eventful life, but at fifty-seven years, you must stop taking decisions on impulse. If the wound had been even an inch deeper, it might have killed you or injured your intestines.'

Smiling apologetically, Zorawar replied, 'Hakim Sahib, I am sorry. My body is no longer as agile as it used to be, but my mind refuses to accept that. Yes, true, that was an impulsive decision and should not have been taken in haste. I will keep that in mind. At fifty-seven, even Zorawar is not what he used to be: "Gajraj of the Battle".'

The hakim lamented, 'Your body is marked with injuries like a colander is riddled with holes. Your wife and children are waiting for you in Kishtwar. You have a duty towards them. Your eldest son, I hear, has grown taller than you and has joined the Sikh regiment under Maharaja Kharak Singh, son of the illustrious Maharaja Ranjit Singh. I know that you have various names:

Lion of the Mountain, Napoleon of the East, etc. But I'm hearing the name "Gajraj of the Battle" for the first time. You might be called Gajraj, but your body cannot take any more strain. You have annexed fort after fort for your king but have ignored your health. Finish this battle and take rest for some time. Believe me, I am your well-wisher and would advise you to call it a day.'

Zorawar agreed, 'You are right. I must finish this battle with the Chinese at To-Yo and return to Kishtwar. It's been so long that I do not remember when my children came of age. I promise that after this battle, I will return to Kishtwar and spend some time with my family.'

Ram Karan exclaimed, 'Oh great General, you have fought so many battles with such bravery that your name will be inscribed in golden letters in the annals of history. But you must not overlook the adverse effects of this cold environment at the Chinese border of To-Yo. A soldier, however loyal he may be to his king, must also take care of his health and family. You have had a long and fruitful life, something not many in this world can say. You must give your body some rest. Can you please tell me about this title I have heard from you for the first time, Gajraj of the Battle?'

Zorawar smiled again and replied, 'Yes, why not Hakim Sahib... Gajraj means the king of elephants. An ancestor of Maharaja Gulab Singh had a huge elephant known as Gajraj. He was so well-trained and powerful that he could create chaos among the enemies all by himself. He was not only obedient but also extremely skilful. In many battles, Gajraj would run amok and instil so much fear in the hearts of enemies that most of the soldiers would flee to save themselves from his fury. There was one time when the enemies got together and plotted to kill Gajraj, but they failed miserably. Their plan to poison him or attack him from all sides did not work. However, one traitor found Gajraj alone and managed to lure him towards quicksand where the king of elephants got trapped and could not free himself. Many soldiers rushed to the area where Gajraj was stuck in quicksand, but they could not help him. A sage passing by suggested that war drums should be beaten and war cries should be raised. The king ordered the soldiers to do as the sage suggested. On hearing the war cries and drums, Gajraj fought with all his remaining strength to pull himself out of the quicksand, narrowly avoiding certain death. The next day on the battlefield, Gajraj took his revenge and rampaged the enemies, using all his might. Maharaja Gulab Singh's ancestor won a decisive battle, thanks to his brave soldiers and the bravest of all—Gajraj.'

Zorawar paused for a while and then said, 'Since I have created chaotic conditions in enemy lines, Maharaja Gulab Singh gave me the title "Gajraj of the Battle".' General Zorawar thanked the hakim, who was tying the knot of his bandage. He gave the hakim some gold coins, which were accepted with gratitude. The hakim was a straightforward man. He cautioned the General, saying, 'You are no longer a young soldier. You are nearing sixty. Think about your age before you embark on such a venture.'

Zorawar replied, 'When faced with difficult times, we must realize that challenges are sent to strengthen us.' The hakim persisted, 'I would still doubt your chances of success in such mindless encounters. What you did was courageous, no doubt, but it could have cost you your life.'

Zorawar dismissed the hakim's doubt, saying, 'Doubt turns all success plans into dust. When pride brings me down, humility raises me up. When cowardice breaks me down, courage lifts me up. When someone pushes me away, God pulls me near to him.'

After the hakim had left, Zorawar found himself reminiscing about his childhood. He recalled a time when he was just six years old, running towards his school in Ansar village, located in the Kangra district, with his friends. Born on 15 April 1784, Zorawar was in the second standard in 1790, when floods engulfed the district. Many people lost their lives, and the school's dilapidated building was swept away. Zorawar and his friend, Prem Singh, had clung to a branch of a tree that could withstand the flow of the water. There had been a cloud burst which had caused devastating floods and landslides in the Kangra district. The heavy rainfall had drained via the river system, inundating all of Ansar village. It was a natural disaster of the worst kind.

Around six thousand habitants of the Kangra district were thought to have died. The destruction of bridges and roads left thousands of locals trapped in the flood. Amidst the raging flood in the village, both the friends clung to a tree, which two monkeys were also stranded on. Zorawar noticed that the monkeys jumped to another tree. Though the tree that the boys held onto seemed firmly rooted in the earth, Zorawar felt apprehensive. Exhibiting wisdom beyond his years, six-year-old Zorawar signalled to Prem that they should jump to the other tree. When Prem objected, Zorawar told him that animals have a sixth sense and can smell danger. As the fury of the flood uprooted the tree they were on, they jumped to the other tree just in time, narrowly avoiding catastrophe.

For two days and one night, the two of them remained without food and water. They were presumed dead by their parents. However, a British army contingent, stationed in the Kangra district, rescued them by throwing ropes at them. The night spent together on the tree had forged a deep bond between Zorawar and Prem that would accompany them on their journey through life. When Zorawar and Prem came of age, they joined the army of Raja Jaswant Singh of Marmotte, better known as the Doda district. Zorawar's exceptional skills in lances and swords were soon noticed by Maharaja Gulab Singh of Jammu, who appointed him as the commandant of the Reasi district.

Zorawar participated in many battles for his ruler and crushed many rebels in the Jammu district. Gulab Singh was so impressed with his feats, sincerity and loyalty that he made Zorawar the governor of Kishtwar and gave him the title of wazir. Zorawar had also served in the army of Maharaja Ranjit Singh and had risen through the ranks as a soldier.

Wazir Zorawar Singh, the Lion of the Mountain, had faced death when he was only six years old. He had a harrowing time while holding onto a branch of a tree for two long days. Such events had a significant impact on him, making him stronger and more determined to succeed in life.

However, those who experience an exponential rise through the ranks have to face hidden enemies. They have to struggle to remain on top since some commanders may be jealous of the rapid promotions earned by someone who had worked under them just a few years earlier. One such scheming, arrogant and unscrupulous commander was Mehtab Khan, who served as one of the commanders of Maharaja Gulab Singh. Mehtab Khan sought to undermine the growing reputation of Zorawar. The maharaja had unshakeable faith in Zorawar and had entrusted him with the fort of Purig in Kargil. Zorawar was also assigned the task of collecting taxes from Purig to Zanskar and from the Gyalpo (king) of Ladakh, who was a subject of Maharaja Gulab Singh.

Mehtab Khan was an astute manipulator who was determined that no one would replace him, always looking for opportunities to malign Zorawar Singh. He became furious when he heard that the king had made Zorawar the wazir of Kishtwar, Riasi Khalsa and Arnas. The king had allowed Zorawar to levy taxes as well as take military action in the region whenever and wherever he deemed necessary. This further enraged Mehtab Khan. He sent a message to one of his trusted lieutenants in the durbar of Maharaja Gulab Singh to plant the seed of suspicion in the ruler's mind regarding the embezzlement of funds by Zorawar in the Kishtwar district. Although the maharaja had no doubts about his wazir, he too was vulnerable to information obtained from a reliable source.

After conducting an investigation, the ruler found that Zorawar's records were clean and impeccable, proving that he had been sincere and honest to the core. Mehtab Khan's move boomeranged on him. It only strengthened the king's trust in Zorawar. Maharaja Gulab Singh personally apologized to Zorawar. It was the first time that such a thing had happened in the state. This was unprecedented. From then on, Zorawar became the favourite wazir of the maharaja. Zorawar had the blessings of God and his king, and he became a force to be reckoned with in Jammu and Kashmir, where the king had apologized to him in front of the court. Mehtab Khan had to swallow the consequences of his actions. Still, he continued to look for another opportunity to belittle Zorawar.

Mehtab once saw a beautiful Hindu girl, Ameera, while on his way to Pulwama in Kashmir. Ameera, who was from the Kishtwar district, was filling water in a utensil from a stream. He ordered his soldiers to abduct the girl to keep her forcibly in his harem. His action was resented by the Hindu sarpanch and a complaint was made to Zorawar. With lightning speed, the wazir entered the palatial *sarai* (rest house), where Mehtab was busy watching nautch girls. Zorawar confronted Mehtab, asking Ameera to be released. The wazir said the girl could not be forced to satisfy Mehtab's lust or be converted to another religion at whim.

When Mehtab Khan refused, Zorawar thrashed him. Ameera was released from his clutches. Mehtab had never been beaten up in front of his subordinates, who did not dare to get involved in the fight. Mehtab had no alternative but to surrender to Zorawar. He returned to his constituency in Ladakh. Mehtab was deeply insulted, and his reputation took a significant blow.

Ameera had a fair complexion and sharp features. Zorawar fell in love with her beauty and charm while taking her to her parents. He tried to contain his emotions, but Ameera's father sensed the wazir's interest in his daughter. He offered Ameera's hand to Zorawar. He told the wazir, 'When you share yourself and your feelings with someone, your life begins to find its meaning. It is only when you touch someone's life that you truly start living. Please accept my daughter as your wife. I have noticed that she has developed a liking for you.'

Zorawar blushed but gathered the courage to say, 'Can this dream be turned into reality? It will certainly pave the way for a glorious future for both of us.' Ameera's father nodded in approval.

After seeking permission from his king, Zorawar and Ameera got married according to the Vedic rites. Three rituals formed an important part of the ceremony: *kanyadaan*, where the father gives away his daughter voluntarily to the bridegroom near the sacred fire to signify union; *panigrahana*, where the bridegroom is allowed to hold the hand of the bride; and *saptapadi*, the seven rounds around the sacred fire taken by the bride and groom while making vows to solemnize the wedding.

The wedding and the elaborate feast were attended by Maharaja Gulab Singh, whose presence added an air of elegance and refinement to the occasion. The ruler bestowed more jaagirs on the wazir. Mehtab was the only commander who was not invited to the feast. He realized that he would either have to get rid of Zorawar or face his wrath. Zorawar had openly declared him his enemy after Ameera's abduction. Mehtab approached the local governor of Ladakh, Gialpo-chi of Timbus—a vassal of the Buddhist Gyalpo of Ladakh, who had earlier lost to Maharaja Gulab Singh, thanks to Zorawar's valour. With the help of Mian Singh, Gialpo-chi, and the Chinese commander, Yang Lee of Xinjiang province, he kidnapped the unsuspecting Zorawar while he was with his wife in Gulmarg. Unaware of the treacherous plot hatched by the Ladakhis, Chinese and Mehtab Khan, Zorawar had been enjoying his leisure time at Gulmarg. Little did he know that he walking into a trap, which was cunningly devised and impossible to foresee.

Zorawar was blindfolded and taken to Skardu Fort in Gilgit-Baltistan. His wife and he were held captive there. Mehtab had connived with Yang Lee to send Zorawar to the gallows. But Maharaja Gulab Singh dispatched his emissaries to Skardu Fort with an offer to release Zorawar for a handsome price of ten thousand gold coins. That was too big a sum for the Chinese commander to refuse. He broke the word he had given to Mehtab and pondered over the release of Zorawar and Ameera.

Yang Lee released Zorawar, grievously injured by the torture, from the fort. Zorawar was taken to the safe haven of the Bhimgarh fort in Reasi. There Zorawar and his wife recovered from the injuries inflicted by the Chinese. He spent his time planning to thwart the revolt of the Gyalpo of Ladakh and kill his arch-enemy, Mehtab Khan. He had decided to deal with Yang Lee later at To-Yo and wrest control of Skardu Fort from him. Zorawar prepared a security force and sent fifty of his trusted men to Ladakh and Skardu Fort. They mingled with the locals and later sent messages about war preparations.

Maharaja Ranjit Singh had been truly impressed by the military prowess, bravery and administrative acumen of Zorawar. On hearing about Mehtab's betrayal, he sent a force of five thousand Sikhs to provide support to the wazir to finish off the rebels in the Ladakh district as well as punish Mehtab, Gialpo-chi and the Chinese. The Ladakhis, under their rebel Gyalpo, had stopped paying their annual tribute and had to be taught a lesson. The tribute paid by the Ladakhis was distributed between Maharaja Gulab Singh and Maharaja Ranjit Singh.

Maharaja Ranjit Singh gave instructions that the entire Ladakh and Kashmir area annexed from Afghanistan in 1819 must be rid of the rebels and the aggressive Chinese. Maharaja Gulab Singh entrusted his wazir with the task of recapturing the forts in the northern parts of Kashmir that were forcibly taken over by Gialpo-chi, the Chinese and Mehtab Khan.

Zorawar quickly recovered from his injuries and led a contingent of ten thousand men along with his commander, Mehta Basti Ram. Their mission was to wrest control of the besieged forts of Kashmir and conquer the higher lands ruled by the Gyalpo and the Chinese in Kargil and the Tibetan sectors. The mountainous region was a difficult terrain, but Zorawar and his soldiers had fought well, overcoming all hurdles. The valiant wazir was satisfied with his campaign and was close to success in killing the traitor of the land who had connived with Yang Lee.

Zorawar was lost in his thoughts when he was brought back to the present by Mehta. The commander offered a helping hand to the injured Zorawar as it was time for him to lead the strong army of Maharaja Ranjit Singh and Maharaja Gulab Singh to reclaim the Ladakh region. Ten thousand soldiers stood ready to unleash mayhem on receiving the signal from the Napoleon of the East.

Seeing Zorawar lead his strong army towards them, the morale of the enemy soldiers plummeted, knowing that their defeat was imminent. With a war cry, Zorawar charged towards Mehtab and the Gyalpo. A pitched battle ensued. Within just an hour, the Gyalpo and Mehtab were killed, and the enemy soldiers surrendered to Zorawar. The entire Ladakh and the strategic Skardu Fort had been conquered once again. Zorawar immediately dispatched a messenger to carry the good news to

Maharaja Gulab Singh and Maharaja Kharak Singh, who had taken over as the ruler of Punjab after the demise of Maharaja Ranjit Singh in 1839.

In 1844, Wazir Zorawar Singh, victor at the age of fifty-seven, prepared for the battle with the Chinese at To-Yo, which was to be his last battle.

SIX

RAISINA HILL

The weather was much colder than usual on the fateful night of 30 January 1941. A dense fog enveloped the entire area around Raisina Hill; it was the part of Delhi where the highest-ranking British officers lived. The Raisina Hill complex had been designed by British architect Edwin Lutyens to rise above its surroundings, giving it a commanding view of the heart of Delhi. It was spread over four square kilometres of land, and one hundred and forty lakh rupees had been spent to turn the vast expanse of land into the estate that housed the governor-general of British India. The estate had two hundred and ninety-eight rooms, an 18-hole golf course and the Mughal Garden, making it the pride of the capital.

Before its revamp, Raisina Hill was a small village that housed three hundred families. The maharaja of Tikamgarh owned the entire estate. The British, on becoming the rulers of India, confiscated the entire land from the maharaja. The British instructed the villagers to shift over to Gurgaon, where land was allotted to them as an alternative plot. A part of Raisina Hill was developed with remarkable architectural work for the residence-cum-office of the governor-general of British India. This estate was later rechristened as the President's Estate.

Nothing quite as magnificent had been built in modern India, and visitors often came to look at it in awe. And yet, on that foggy night, it stirred an ominous feeling of impending danger and death. There was hardly any traffic. Only a black-coloured Buick car with three occupants moved towards the estate. The occupants—Javed Khan, Pratap Singh Rajput and Fatima Begum—were visibly tense, and Fatima kept looking back to see if they were being followed. No one spoke a word. They had received information that the maharaja of Tikamgarh had found out through his spies that Fatima and her paramour were hiding with Pratap's relatives in Civil Lines, Delhi. They had betrayed the powerful ruler, and any kind of betrayal against him meant certain death. The British never interfered in the personal affairs of the rulers of the princely states, as long as they were loyal to them. The occupants of the Buick had no reason to ask for any protection from the law enforcers. They were planning to escape towards Gurgaon and then move on to the Pataudi road to take refuge with another one of Pratap's relatives, an obscure farmer in the Harsaru village. There was no time to be lost. They knew that the maharaja was a ruthless and vengeful person who would not let such a betrayal go unpunished. The threat had intensified when Pratap noticed one of the goons of the maharaja moving around the Civil Lines area.

The Buick accelerated to its maximum possible speed and was barely a hundred feet away from the main entrance to the estate when it attempted to make a right turn onto the road that would take them towards Dhaula Kuan, leading then to Gurgaon and, hopefully, to safety. Suddenly, a fast-moving grey-coloured car that seemed to appear out of nowhere hit the Buick with all its force. There was a deafening sound. In a flash, five men wearing turbans, their faces covered with silk scarves, stepped out of the grey car and surrounded the shaken passengers of the Buick. Armed with pistols, knives and swords, they attempted to pull Fatima out of the wreckage. They had their instructions: kidnap and bring back the woman and assassinate both her paramour, Javed, and his accomplice, Pratap.

When Pratap and Javed tried to protect Fatima, they had to face a barrage of bullets. Both ducked behind the car, stunned by the ferocity of the assault on them. Javed, an ex-aide of Maharaja Ranbir Singh, pulled out a service revolver that he was carrying and fired back at the assailants. A bullet hit one of the attackers in the chest, and as blood oozed out of the wound, his grip on the woman loosened. Javed quickly moved closer in an attempt to rescue her, and a further exchange of fire followed. Before long, Javed exhausted all of his bullets.

Seeing his chance, one of the assailants, the tallest and most daring amongst them, drew out a sword and charged at Javed and Pratap. His accomplice took out his knife as well and both ran towards the three unfortunate passengers of the Buick as they cowered behind the badly damaged car, trying desperately to protect themselves.

Fatima, wounded and bleeding, began shouting for help even as the assailant with the sword caught up with Javed and tried to slash his throat. Both Javed and Pratap realized that there was no escape. It was now a matter of life and death. Javed, who had been trained for personal combat, ducked and swung at the assailant with considerable force. The two of them fought valiantly, taking the attackers by surprise. But there were only two of them against five of the assailants. They were outnumbered. Seizing the opportunity, the burly, muscular and blood thirsty goons of the maharaja cornered the two victims. One fired a volley of bullets that pierced the right shoulder of Javed. The revolver fell from his hand with the gnawing pain of the bullets finding their mark. One of the assailants thrust his knife into Javed's neck, instantly rupturing an artery. His eyes bulged out in shock and a fountain of blood spurted from his neck too. Within seconds, Javed was dead.

The assailants, who had been assigned the task to kill both the traitors, now moved toward Pratap to finish him off as well. Just then, another car drove up to the scene of the crime and three British officers—Lt Smith, Lt Bailey and Lt Francis Stephen—stepped out of their car to try and help the victims. They were returning after a game of billiards at a nearby club in Connaught Place. Pratap, who had received several knife injuries and was bleeding profusely, was still trying to defend himself. On seeing the British officers, the assailants froze and then attempted to escape as quickly as they could. To be caught with a dead man would have meant either a scandal or a prolonged prison sentence. While the British did not care about the number of wives the Indian royalty had or the harems they maintained, a dead body was quite another matter. Three of the five assailants managed to jump into their car and speed away. The other two, finding themselves in a precarious situation, tried to run in opposite directions. Before doing so, one of them thrust his sword into Pratap's stomach and leaving the sword there, ran after his accomplice. The British army officers pursued the two assailants and soon overpowered them. The three officers were from the British Armed Forces and were well-trained in combat.

The two assailants arrested by the British officers were Sawanth Rathore and Jaswant Krishna, and as it turned out, both were residents and employees of Maharaja Ranbir Singh, ruler of the vast princely state of Tikamgarh. While Pratap succumbed to his injuries, Fatima, the main target of the attack, survived. She recorded her statement at the Tughlaq Road Police Station and later in the British Court, in what turned out to be one of the most publicized royal scandals.

The incident and the entire story of Fatima were splashed across the front page of the newspaper.

Fatima Begum was born in Kabul and grew up to be a breathtakingly beautiful woman with light hazel eyes and long auburn hair. Her beauty and gentleness had mesmerized many men. She came from a poor family in Kabul that left her with only a few choices. As life would have it, she landed, at the age of seventeen, as a dancer in the harem of Maharaja Ranbir Singh of Tikamgarh in Rajasthan. Though there were three hundred and sixty women in the maharaja's harem, Fatima soon became his favourite. He was obsessed with her beauty and lavished her with gifts and attention. However, her life was nothing more than that of a slave, obliged as she was to obey every whim of the cruel maharaja. He owned her for all purposes.

After ten years in the maharaja's harem, at the age of twenty-seven, Fatima could take it no more. Two things happened: she fell madly in love with the maharaja's aide, Javed Khan, and, secondly, she took the help of Maharani Satibai, the maharaja's senior wife, to escape from the harem. When she had an affair with Javed and then eloped with him, she had practically signed her death warrant. After they had escaped from Tikamgarh, they reached Delhi and sought the help of Javed's childhood friend, Pratap Singh Rajput, who in turn had arranged shelter for them at the home of his distant cousin. Thus, Pratap also became an accomplice and was instrumental in helping them escape from the clutches of the maharaja.

Pratap himself was of royal blood, but unlike Maharaja Ranbir Singh, he was a principled and pious man. His ancestors had been warriors and had ruled a small state in Rajasthan's Jhalawar district before the Mughal army ran over them. They accepted the sovereignty of the Mughal emperor Shah Alam II in the eighteenth century as well as of the last Mughal emperor, Bahadur Shah Zafar. Later on, they settled in Delhi in the jaagir (estate) allotted to them in Civil Lines by Bahadur Shah Zafar.

They also had massive farmlands on the outskirts of Pataudi. Once a Rajput accepts a fugitive, the custom demands that he protect the couple that has taken shelter under him.

When Maharaja Ranbir Singh got to know of his mistress's affair and her daring escape, he was outraged. He saw it as an affront to his royal dignity. The eunuchs guarding the harem informed him that Fatima had lately begun to openly curse the maharaja. These betrayals would not be forgiven. He sought vengeance. He would either drag the bloody dancer back to his harem to avenge the insult or, if that was not possible, do away with her—revenge or death. This would be a show of strength for him and also a warning to anyone else who dared to think of disobedience. He had issued orders to his men to finish off Javed, who had once been his trusted aide, and the two Rajput brothers who had betrayed him by giving shelter to Fatima in Delhi.

Fatima was seventeen when she had been sold to the maharaja in 1914 for a hundred gold coins. Smitten with her beauty, he pampered her with gifts and special favours. He couldn't take his eyes off her. He was so infatuated with her that despite having seventeen wives, he chose to spend his leisure time only with Fatima. The other women in his harem were treated very badly. He would often beat them cruelly if they failed to satisfy his lust.

He had recently turned fifty-six and virtually ignored his wives and the other dancers. As his obsession with Fatima grew, he showered her with more and more expensive jewellery, gifting her one precious necklace after another, making the other women in the harem jealous. One by one, they turned against Fatima.

Maharani Satibai too noticed the change in her husband and gradually an idea took shape in her mind. She conspired to kill two birds with one stone. She zeroed in on the most handsome aide of her husband, Javed, and began sending him across regularly to Fatima with one message or another. She created every opportunity for the two to be together. The plan worked like a charm. Javed and Fatima fell in love, and Maharani Satibai encouraged them to escape to a place where they would not be found by the maharaja.

Javed had spent nine years serving under the maharaja and had a jaagir of his own in Tikamgarh, a gift from the maharaja. Still, he had come to despise the maharaja for his cruelty towards his subjects. The maharaja was unscrupulous and lived only for himself, never showing any interest in the welfare of his subjects. His cruelty bordered on sadism. He, however, had one source of constant concern. He had many wives but no heir apparent, something he blamed his wives for. Without an heir, his regime would come to an end. The British would not let his widows inherit his estate, and everything he owned would be usurped by them. That is what had happened with the Rani of Jhansi, and that is what would happen to his kingdom too. The law laid down by the British was clear. In case there was no legal heir, the collected taxes would go to the British and no princely allowances would be given to the widows of the deceased. They would then have to fend for themselves. This meant that they would eventually have to sell what they owned and do away with the employees who were at their beck and call.

The maharaja had his hopes in Fatima. She would bear him a son. Even though the French doctors had told him that he could never become a father, he chose to believe the fakirs and astrologers who proclaimed that he would indeed become a father, to a handsome son born of a foreign mistress. The only mistress of foreign origin in his harem was Fatima, who had come from Kabul. He was convinced that she was the one to give him a child. He would even marry her with such an arrangement to make their child a legitimate legal heir and Fatima, his eighteenth queen.

And to think that this woman, this Fatima, whom he had

cherished and pampered, and from whom he had such high hopes for an heir, had run away under his nose—and that too with his own trusted aide. It was a double betrayal and unbearable for him. He was furious. He had sent a team of assailants after them but the plot to abduct her and bring her back to him had been foiled due to the intervention of the three British army lieutenants.

Both Javed and Pratap had been killed on the night of 30 January at Raisina Hill. The British police posted a few guards outside the home of Pratap's cousin, who had sheltered the couple, to protect him from the wrath of Maharaja Ranbir Singh, who was likely to go after him too. The maharaja had indeed sent a team of four men to finish him off. However, seeing the police guards outside his home, they bided their time. A month or so later, assuming the danger was now past, the police officers were told to disband from the post. Soon after, the four men entered the house in Civil Lines, where Javed and Fatima had laid hidden for several months. Within minutes, Pratap's cousin was dead, and the killers were on their way back to Tikamgarh, leaving behind not even an iota of evidence. They had strangulated him and then hanged him on a ceiling fan to give the impression of a suicide. Some antidepressants were left on the table nearby to suggest that he was under acute depression.

Meanwhile, the two assailants who had been arrested on the night of 30 January were tried in a court of law. Under police pressure, they revealed that the entire plot had been hatched by the maharaja. Their instructions were to kill Javed and his friend as well as kidnap Fatima and bring her to the maharaja. They got the order to kill her too, if needed. They pleaded mercy since they had only been acting on the orders of their ruler. Fatima was summoned by the court to identify the assailants. On her testimony, the court sentenced both of them to death.

One fallout of the assassination attempt was that Maharaja

Ranbir Singh was forced to abdicate his throne to his younger brother Karan Singh, who became the caretaker ruler of the Tikamgarh district, working under the aegis of the British government which presided over India. He remained a subject of the British but was allowed only a portion of the tax collected by the British from his estate to maintain himself and his estate.

The defence lawyers of the assailants appealed to the Privy Council for clemency, arguing that the two men were acting on behalf of their employer. Their arguments failed to move the court. The judges claimed that it was a planned murder. The death sentence was affirmed.

The other three assailants were still at large. Despite several raids by the British police, they had not been caught. It was rumoured that the maharaja had had them killed. No one ever heard from them or saw them again.

The case became famous and photographs of Fatima and the accused were splashed across all the mainstream newspapers. A leading newspaper called it 'The Raisina Hill Murder'. The term stuck and newspapers all over the country echoed it. The Raisina Hill murder turned out to be the scandal of the decade. Sensation-hungry media reporters followed every court proceeding and covered every appearance of the accused and Fatima.

The death sentence judgment was analysed in detail by newspapers and the radio; expert opinions were sought. The media dwelt upon every detail of the scandal. A dancer in a harem had defied and insulted a maharaja. Five people died as a result: Javed, Pratap, his cousin, and two of the assailants. There was enough vengeance, jealousy and passion to keep the newspapers churning news about the murders day after day. The case became the talk of the town.

Two months after the gory incident in which the person she loved most in the world had died, Fatima discovered that she was pregnant and carrying his child. She reflected on her time with the maharaja and the aversion she felt when he touched her. And how different it was with Javed—how his touch simultaneously aroused her and soothed her. Initially, Javed lent her a sympathetic ear. Eventually, the relationship transformed into a kind of love she had never known. The months they had spent hiding together in a remote part of Delhi had been the best period of her life.

Neither Fatima nor Javed had any inkling about the strength of the maharaja's faith in the prophecy that a foreign woman would bear his child. And that this prophecy had made her a coveted possession of the maharaja. When Javed took her away, the maharaja lost not just the woman he was infatuated with but also his potential heir. It was an act that hit him where it hurt most. For four months, the maharaja sent his spies to find them but to no avail. Until that night in January.

After several months in hiding, Fatima asked Javed to show her India Gate. Although initially reluctant and trying to dissuade her, Javed ultimately agreed. They left for India Gate in a horse carriage.

That same evening, one of the maharaja's spies happened to be present at India Gate, and despite Fatima wearing a burqa and Javed having shaved off his beard, he recognized them. He followed them to their residence in Civil Lines, and the next morning, the maharaja knew where the two lovers were hiding. It was time to take his revenge and bring back his mistress, who would later give him an heir, proving the astrologers right.

The plot to punish the three rebels was hatched. The maharaja had decided that he wanted the men killed but not Fatima. He wanted her abducted and brought back to him as he was still holding on to the hope that she would provide him with a son. Things were going according to plan but the intervention of the three British army officers threw everything into chaos.

Things had begun to unravel for Maharaja Ranbir Singh. Fatima had not been returned to him and his last hopes of getting a son and heir were ruined. Moreover, his image had been tarnished, and there were whisper campaigns against him. In hushed tones, people insinuated that he had Javed and the upright Pratap killed. The murder of Pratap's innocent cousin was widely criticized. The newspapers continued to write damning articles about the maharaja's misdeeds.

The depressed maharaja considered moving out of the country. He quietly sold some of his properties in Tikamgarh to shady but influential buyers. He also sold some of his valuables to a famous jeweller in Delhi. He transferred the hefty amount he received from these sales to Paris. He bought a villa on the outskirts of Paris and moved there with four of his queens. He had decided never to come back to India. His younger brother was declared the new maharaja of Tikamgarh, making him lose all his power.

Meanwhile, Fatima was left with few choices. The man she loved had been killed. She had no money and nowhere to go. The only asset she had was the jewellery that had been gifted to her by the maharaja, which she had taken with her when she had escaped from his harem. She finally moved into a small room at Griffins Hotel in Connaught Place. The hotel was run by a British widow called Angela Griffins. On the ground floor, she ran a bakery, and on the first floor, the hotel. Angela Griffin took a liking to Fatima, and it was with her support that Fatima slowly recovered from her trauma and began to regain some of her physical and mental strength. On 30 September 1941, she gave birth to a baby boy.

As the days passed, the two women grew closer. Fatima slowly shared with Mrs Griffins her issues and plight. Mrs Griffins suggested that she name the baby after the man she had loved. Fatima refused to do so at first. Memories of that terrible night at Raisina Hill still haunted her. She did not want to ever think about all the things she had lost that night, nor did she want her son to ever know about her past life of being a mistress of Maharaja Ranbir Singh. She would have to make up a story for him when he grew up and began asking questions. Still, on Mrs Griffins' insistence, she named her son 'Javed'.

Mrs Griffins proposed that Fatima help her run the hotel and bakery, and, in exchange, she could stay in the room free of cost and simultaneously look after her child. Mrs Griffins had grown very fond of the good looks and innocence of the toddler. Since she was a childless widow, the presence of little Javed helped fill a deep void in her life. She doted on him.

Meanwhile, the world had gone through a really bad phase due to the Second World War. India was rapidly changing. When Javed turned six, Fatima took him to Princess Park to witness a historic moment. It was 15 August 1947, and the Indian flag was unfurled for the first time. India was a free country at last. These were heady and historic times, and Fatima wanted her son to witness them. The next day, she took him to the Red Fort where the first prime minister of India, Jawaharlal Nehru, raised the Indian flag on the ramparts of the Red Fort. She told Javed the story of India's struggle for independence that began with the mutiny of a handful of soldiers led by Mangal Pandey in 1857 and reached its climax with Mahatma Gandhi's policy of non-violence against the British. The Red Fort was the spot chosen for the lowering of the British flag and the raising of the Indian flag since it was symbolic of the crowning of the last Mughal emperor, Bahadur Shah Zafar, and the declaration of Independence by the rebel sepoys, even though it was short-lived and lasted only a few months. The unfurling of the flag at the Red Fort was done against the wishes of the last viceroy of India, but there it was. India was a free country and after ninety years of struggle, the

British flag was finally lowered. It was thrilling for young Javed to see these changes as well as gain access to the sprawling, 255-acre Red Fort, where so much history had unfolded.

One fallout of India's independence was that Mrs Griffins, like many other British people, decided to leave India. She had been shaken by the Hindu-Muslim riots of 1947 and the carnage and anti-British sentiments that followed. It seemed best for her to sell the hotel and bakery and leave the country forever.

But before she was to leave, she made an unusual request that shook Fatima to the core. Mrs Griffins wanted to adopt Javed and take him to London with her.

The request came as a big shock. Fatima's life had finally begun to have a measure of contentment after the turmoil of her earlier days. At Griffins Hotel, she found a sense of home and formed a nurturing friendship with the owner, Mrs Griffins. Her son's admission into a unique school close to the hotel was an added benefit. He had been going to Modern School on Barakhamba Road for the last two years. The school was spread over 26 acres of land, and the curriculum focussed on the all-round development of students. Fatima's child was thriving and was also liked by his teachers. He had made some good friends and was enjoying his time in school.

The two assailants who had been convicted were finally hanged. The murder of Fatima's beloved had partly been avenged, though the main culprit was roaming free in France. Still, Fatima felt a kind of peace. But now, with this new development, everything seemed to be slipping away. Her home, her friend, and even her son gone? No, she could not let that happen. She could not lose her son.

Mrs Griffins tried to convince her. She said that if Javed continued to stay in India, one day he would surely discover the truth about his mother. That she was a dancer in a harem and mistress to a maharaja. That she eloped with another man, and five people died in the events that followed. Her son would never be able to live a normal life after coming to know about her past.

She convinced Fatima that it would be best for her to remarry and settle down. After all, she was only thirty-three years old and still so beautiful. Someone out there would be happy to be with her despite her sordid background. And she could rest assured that her beloved child would be looked after well. Mrs Griffins would rechristen him Harry, the name of her late husband, and she would ensure that his schooling and further education would happen in the finest institutions that London had to offer. Letting him go would be the biggest gift Fatima could give her child. The moment he set foot in London, a bright future awaited him.

Fatima asked for a few days to decide. It was the hardest decision she had ever had to make. It would be a turning point and would change her life forever. Life without her child was unthinkable. However, she realized that such an opportunity may not come again. Mrs Griffins loved Javed and would take good care of him. She would give him access to a life that Fatima never could. True, her son could perhaps land a government job in India when he grew up, but that did not compare with what he could get in London. There he would one day inherit the vast estate that belonged to Mrs Griffins. Moreover, he would be spared the knowledge of his mother's dark past.

With a heavy heart, Fatima agreed to Mrs Griffins' proposal. Javed would become Mrs Griffins' son, and he would be renamed Harry.

Mrs Griffins was delighted. She sold her bakery and hotel to Mr B.M. Tandon, a well-known businessman in Delhi, with the condition that he continue to employ Fatima for at least ten years. Mr Tandon, like most people in Delhi, had read about the Raisina Hill murder case. Even years later, people talked about it. Nevertheless, he agreed to Mrs Griffins' proposal and closed the deal. Fatima could continue to work and stay in the hotel.

With tears in her eyes, Fatima bade farewell to her only child at the railway station. The train was to take him and Mrs Griffin to Bombay, from where they would catch a ship to Dover port in the United Kingdom. Fatima realized with a sudden shock that this was the last time she would see him as Javed. If they ever met again, he would be Harry Griffins.

For Mrs Griffins, it would be a return to her home after almost twenty-five years. They took the ship from Bombay which docked at the Dover port. From there, they took a train to London's Waterloo station and then took a taxi to Belsize Avenue, where Mrs Griffins' parents once lived. They had passed away but the lavish house had been kept in mint condition by their capable old housekeeper, Gloria.

Mrs Griffins noticed that a lot had changed in the years she had been away in India. The subway system was now spread out like a web over almost all of London. It had become more expensive after the Second World War, but it could get you to almost any location in London with great ease.

After settling down in their new home, Mrs Griffins took Harry everywhere to acquaint him with the city in which he was to spend the rest of his life. She was delighted to show him around. She took him to Buckingham Palace, the Tower of London, the British Museum and Trafalgar Square. She took him to see Big Ben and on a cruise on the River Thames. She wanted to give him a feel of London, and six-year-old Harry took it all in with wide-eyed wonder. He fell in love with London; he hadn't seen anything like it. He was baptized in the church and the six-year-old Javed thence became a Griffins—Harry Griffins, son of Angela and the (Late) Harry Griffins.

Young Harry was admitted to Bramley Towers School in

Fulham, and with everything being so new and thrilling, he soon began to forget about his life in Delhi and its small bylanes. He forgot about the mayhem caused by the riots during Partition. He recalled some houses burning in an area and some discussions about a large number of people going to Pakistan, but he couldn't quite understand it. Much of it was a blur. He did remember the soft touch of his mother and the security he felt as he slept curled up in her arms. Mrs Griffin, however, cared for him so much that he forgot his past and became a British citizen.

Studies and games kept Harry occupied, and he eventually forgot most things about India. He grew into a tall and handsome young man who studied law at the same university as Sardar Patel, the first home minister of India, with the goal of becoming a lawyer. He became a first-class lawyer. In every way—manner, etiquette and dressing style—Harry was British. And yet, despite spending eighteen years in London, something within him remained Indian.

By that time, Mrs Griffins was eighty-four and gravely ill with cancer. She put up a fight but, like most dying people, knew from instinct that her days were numbered. Before it was too late, she knew there was something she must do.

Three critical things happened to Harry on that fateful day in 1965, before Mrs Griffin passed away. It was nearly twenty-four years after the Raisina Hill murders. Mrs Griffin called her son to her deathbed and revealed to him the secret she had kept hidden from him all these years. She told a shocked Harry that his real mother was Fatima Begum and that she was very much alive and lived in Delhi. She gave him Fatima's latest address. Harry could not believe his ears. He had a faint memory of a beautiful woman showering him with love and kisses when he was a child. But he had been told by his foster mother that the woman had died during the Partition riots. Harry knew that he had been adopted, but he had always been told that he was an orphan. Although he had received much love from his foster mother, the revelation that he was not an orphan and that his mother was alive left him stunned.

The second thing he learned that night was that he would inherit a large estate after his foster mother's death. The home they lived in was vast and luxurious. There was also a large amount of money that he had not been aware of. Now all of that would go to him. He could buy several homes or any number of cars, one to match each of his outfits, if he was so inclined. He was set to inherit all of his foster mother's properties and bank balances, making him a wealthy man. He had inherited government bonds yielding six per cent interest for five million pounds.

It was snowing heavily in London. The temperature was below minus ten degrees. Harry stepped out to make sense of all that he had been told. When he came back, his foster mother was gone. He walked around the house in a daze, not sure what to do. He kept expecting a door to open and Mrs Griffins to walk in as usual. But it was not to be. He absent-mindedly opened a drawer in her room and stumbled upon an old diary, and that is when he found out all about the Raisina Hill murder, exactly twenty-four years ago on 30 January. That was the third big thing that was revealed to him on that fateful night.

Three big revelations in a single day. Harry sat down to take it all in. He randomly opened the diary on a page, and found a yellow newspaper cutting describing the Raisina Hill case. He read the entire article twice. Slowly, everything became crystal clear to him. He now knew his real mother's name and the sacrifices she had made. He also learned about the viciousness of the man who had held her prisoner for many years, Maharaja Ranbir Singh of Tikamgarh.

On that night, Harry, for the first time as an adult, saw the photograph of a beautiful twenty-seven-year-old woman, his mother. He learned that his father had been murdered at Raisina Hill. And he learned simultaneously who the murderer was.

Harry arranged for his foster mother's burial with full dignity, and he performed all the last rites of a son. After that, he went to the British Council Library in Central London where he dug up every available piece of information on the Raisina Hill murder case. News reports going back decades were neatly archived and every minute detail of the infamous murder case was available in the voluminous crime section archives of the library.

He discovered that his father was Javed Khan, and that he had fought bravely with the assailants before he was stabbed to death. He discovered that Maharaja Ranbir Singh, the cruel and cowardly ruler of Tikamgarh, had sent the assailants. The case had become the scandal of the year. The British authorities had become involved, and the case had even made its way into the British press. And, finally, he learned that Maharaja Ranbir Singh had been forced to abdicate his throne to his younger brother Karan Singh.

Harry was struck by the many layers of cruelty displayed by the maharaja, who was not only willing to kill numerous people to take revenge for a personal affront, but even ready to kill his once-cherished mistress if the abduction was not possible.

Barrister Harry reviewed the case with his sharp legal mind. He felt that the British authorities had been much too lenient with the maharaja by simply allowing him to abdicate his throne. A more fitting punishment would have been death by hanging. He made his notes and then decided to seek further advice from lawyers in New Delhi.

He reflected on the discrimination practised by the British when they ruled over India. Bhagat Singh and two others had been hanged for killing Inspector Sanders, a British police officer, while

Maharaja Ranbir Singh, the ruler of an insignificant state, who was responsible for three deaths, was let off so easily—primarily because his victims were Indian. Not only had he been allowed to leave for Paris, he had also managed to take all his jewellery and money with him. Harry hit the desk in the library with his fist at the injustice of it all. He meant to make it his life's mission to restore justice, which, in this case, was to avenge the murder of his father.

A week later he was on a flight to Delhi. The plane landed at Palam Airport, which had been newly built as the old Safdarjung Airport was no longer found to be viable for large planes and international flights. He got into a taxi with an address in hand: 108 Hind Park, Daryaganj. On the way, his taxi crossed India Gate, where he stopped for a minute to see the majestic Raisina Hill sweeping upward like a commanding presence. Harry felt a strange mix of emotions at what had happened and a feeling that he could not yet decipher. He was about to meet his mother.

He got out of the taxi in Daryaganj and rang the bell. A woman in her mid-fifties opened the door. She had a tinge of white in her hair but was still very beautiful. She looked at her son, now six feet tall, who looked handsome and fresh even after a long, tiring journey from London. They stood looking at each other in silence for a few minutes.

Then she moved forward and embraced him, tears running down her face. The tears wouldn't stop. She was choked with emotion. She told him that, for a moment, she thought she was dreaming. Harry looked so much like his father—the same height, the same fair complexion and the same eyes—a replica but for the accent.

Fatima took Harry inside her small three-room flat. While she went into the kitchen to make tea for him, he splashed water on his face. The washroom was in a corner of an open courtyard.

When they finally sat down to talk, there was too much to catch up on. Fatima told him that despite Mrs Griffins' advice, she had not remarried and had continued to work in the hotel. Mrs Griffins, true to her word, had kept Fatima informed of what her son was doing. She had also sent him photographs of Harry on each of his birthdays. Fatima brought them out, her collection of photographs of Harry ever since he was a small child. They told the saga of the last twenty-four years.

Harry decided to move his mother to a brand-new colony being developed at Greater Kailash in South Delhi. He was rich enough to provide a decent home for his mother. As he scanned the newspaper listings every day to find a large house in Greater Kailash, he stumbled upon a news report on the Maharaja of Tikamgarh. Harry read the report with growing interest. It mentioned that a twenty-year-old case involving properties, worth millions of pounds, of the rulers of Tikamgarh, had been finally concluded. The order had been passed in favour of the exiled ex-ruler of Tikamgarh, Ranbir Singh. The report also went on to state that his younger brother, Karan Singh, had pleaded that all the properties, including the 20-acre Tikamgarh House in Lutyens' Delhi, legally belonged to him after Ranbir Singh had been forced to abdicate the throne in his favour.

The court had passed the order in the exiled maharaja's favour due to one missing document that was the vital piece of evidence in the case: the ordinance for the abdication. This was a simple two-page order that had mysteriously gone missing from the files and archives at the Central Secretariat. Everything hinged on that ordinance, and now it was gone. The maharaja had claimed that he had willingly gone over to France, and there was no abdication in favour of Karan Singh.

Karan Singh tried his level best to look for the evidence but nothing was available—neither with him nor in any government records. Without that piece of paper, Karan Singh did not have a legal leg to stand on and half the properties were awarded to the exiled maharaja. The last column of the news report stated that Maharaja Karan Singh had been disappointed, but after putting up a fight, had decided to surrender the properties and had shown no inclination to file an appeal against the orders. The values of the properties had gone up so high that he was content with just the half portion awarded to him by the High Court of Rajasthan.

Harry flinched at the injustice. The wicked murderer of his father and the man who had ruined his mother's life had been living in luxury in Paris all these years. He deserved to die. Instead, he would soon become the owner of some of the most valuable real estate in Lutyens' Delhi.

Enough was enough… Harry could not let this injustice continue. Fatima noticed his agitation and asked him to proceed in a cool-headed manner if he wanted to truly ensure that the culprit got his comeuppance.

Harry drew up a plan. He went to the law firm Palkhivala & Palkhivala, which had been handling the matter on behalf of Maharaja Karan Singh. He met Mr Rustam Palkhivala and offered to work in his law firm as a junior advocate. To his surprise, Rustam had heard about Harry. He had read about a particularly complex case about a bank heist in London that Harry had fought and resolved. The case had been a tricky one with many loopholes, and the way that Harry had argued it had drawn the attention of the media. This had brought Harry and the law firm where he worked, Fairway Legal Eagles, widespread fame. Rustam, one of the senior-most lawyers in India, often attended courts in London and was quite familiar with the law firm in which Harry worked. He was delighted to have Harry in his team.

Harry said he was especially interested in the Tikamgarh properties case and that they should try to convince Maharaja

Karan Singh to file an appeal against the order awarding half of his properties to the exiled Ranbir Singh, who had used treachery and guile to make the ordinance document disappear.

But Karan Singh was not keen on pursuing the case. He had been diagnosed with cancer and the doctors had given him a year, a maximum of two, to live. He did not want to spend them tied up in legal battles. Meanwhile, the lawyers of Ranbir Singh had already moved to claim Tikamgarh House on Crescent Road. That property alone was worth crores.

Harry tried again to convince Karan Singh. This was injustice, he said. If not for himself, for the sake of justice, he should file an appeal in the Supreme Court of India. After some hesitation, Karan Singh agreed to Harry's proposition.

Seeing some hope, Harry prepared the draft appeal himself and got it approved by the senior team at Palkhivala & Palkhivala and filed it with the Supreme Court of India. His petition was so persuasive that the division bench judges of the Supreme Court admitted the petition, and the case was listed for hearing after a month.

Later that day, Harry went to see the Crescent Road property. It stretched out towards Raisina Hill, where twenty-four years ago, Ranbir Singh had ordered the murder of his father. Staring at the spot, he was more determined than ever to avenge the dastardly crime that had forced his mother into a lifetime of servitude.

The next day, a meeting was convened at the law offices of Palkhivala & Palkhivala and the case *Ranbir Singh vs Karan Singh* was thrashed out, each pro and con closely examined. Maharaja Karan Singh had regained his motivation to fight the case and expressed his concern about the missing document; the ordinance was the most important piece of evidence and crucial to winning the case.

Maharaja Karan Singh had stated categorically that the ordinance was passed by the British Government in April 1942. He had kept the copy thereof in his safe for more than twenty long years, but it mysteriously disappeared. It had either been genuinely misplaced or, more likely, intentionally removed from the records. What to do next? Harry surprised everyone by saying that he had already booked a flight to London to try and locate a copy of the original ordinance which may be in the British Government records. He said that though Mr Lawrence, the former prime minister, had retired and so had Lord Metcalfe, he was willing to take the chance to go to London and try and recover the ordinance or at least find some proof that it existed. His confidence was infectious. The entire team pinned their hopes on Harry.

Before he left for London, Harry had one thing to do. He had found his mother a new independent house in Greater Kailash. After ensuring that she was comfortably settled, he left for London. On landing, he made his enquiries and found out that the former prime minister, now in his eighties, was staying in Sussex. Harry left for Sussex immediately and managed to get an appointment with him. Lawrence listened to Harry's story about the Raisina Hill case, one that he recalled in considerable detail, and referred him to Sir John Macaulay who, he believed, had or could source a copy of the ordinance. Harry was in luck. Within a couple of days, he had a copy of the ordinance in his hand. He smiled. This would clinch the case. He had requested for the original to be given over to him but that request was rejected by Sir John Macaulay.

But even before he landed in Delhi, word had reached Ranbir Singh that a young lawyer from London named Harry had been taking a lot of interest in the case. His lawyer informed him that Harry had managed to source a copy of the ordinance. With that document, Ranbir Singh's right to the Crescent Road property, as well as all the other properties, could be in jeopardy. Ranbir

Singh was furious at this development. Who was this young lawyer and why was he so interested in this case? Ranbir Singh, now seventy-six, could not afford to lose the Crescent Road property. He had incurred millions in debt while living in Paris with his extravagant lifestyle and was now almost bankrupt. Without the proceeds from selling this property, he could be in severe legal trouble in Paris.

Ranbir Singh's first thoughts were to meet the young lawyer and perhaps bribe him over to his side. But his lawyers informed him that Harry had an impeccable reputation and total integrity towards his clients, and this strategy probably would backfire. Another plan was needed to protect his interests and soon, Ranbir Singh came up with it, a plan to extricate the copy of the ordinance that would, for once and for all, close the matter in favour of Karan Singh.

Harry landed a day later at Palam Airport, triumphantly carrying the copy of the original ordinance certificate with him. This would nail the exiled murderer and get a favourable order from the Supreme Court to Maharaja Karan Singh. It would now be only a matter of days.

But Harry was in for a surprise. No sooner had he alighted from the aircraft, than he saw four customs officers heading towards him. Intuitively, he sensed a trap. His sharp legal brain knew he needed to protect the ordinance. Pretending he needed to urgently visit the washroom before proceeding with them, he quickly sealed the certificate in a plastic bag and hid it behind the cistern in the washroom. As soon as he came out of the washroom, he was whisked away to the customs' office by the four officers. He was asked to wait till a senior officer came to interrogate him. Harry knew that this could only be the handiwork of Ranbir Singh, who must have used his money and connections to sabotage the case.

After keeping him waiting for an hour, during which he was not allowed to even move, a senior customs officer walked in. He was accompanied by Mohammed Suleiman, a trusted aide of Ranbir Singh. It was Suleiman who did the talking. He spoke aggressively to Harry and asked him to hand over the certificate and only then they would let him go. He was threatened with dire consequences if he failed to do so.

Harry stood up and looked Suleiman firmly in the eye and stated that he was a British citizen and nobody could compel him to answer any questions or divulge any details that had nothing to do with customs and excise laws. He knew his rights, and he knew the law. He turned to the senior customs officer, who was a stooge of Ranbir Singh, and stated that he was a barrister and would take him to court for this confinement, which was illegal, unwarranted, incompetent and unjustified in the eyes of the law.

The customs officer smiled condescendingly and said that though Harry may be a British citizen, he may still be carrying contraband, and if he did not want to be implicated and charged, he had better hand over the certificate to Suleiman. Harry responded with anger and a threat. If the officer dared illegally slip any contraband into his suitcase, Harry would not let the matter be. He would use his full legal force to take him to court.

Harry's outburst was intentional, knowing fully well that it would provoke a reaction in the senior official. As he had anticipated, the official was furious. How dare this chit of a young man speak to him so rudely? He ordered his subordinates to grab him and hit him hard. One of the junior customs officers hit Harry with full force. Harry fell bleeding from the cut on his nose.

Suleiman again came menacingly towards him and asked him to hand over the certificate. Else, the ex-Maharaja was still powerful enough to see him rot in jail for many years on the charges of smuggling of contraband goods.

Harry stood up and cleaned the blood from his lips, saying with conviction that the information received by them was incorrect, that despite his trying his very best, he had not managed to obtain the certificate. They were welcome to open his suitcase and verify this for themselves. There was sincerity in his voice that confused Suleiman and the customs officers present. Suleiman retorted that his suitcases had already been checked. Now, they were going to check him since he had likely hidden the certificate on his person. He barked at the customs officer, asking them to go ahead and frisk him thoroughly.

Harry pretended indignation as they frisked him. Suleiman was still not convinced that Harry was telling the truth. He questioned him about a phone call he had made three days ago to the Palkhivala & Palkhivala law offices telling them he had obtained the certificate. The former maharaja had a mole in their office. Neither the suitcase nor the body search had shown any certificate. Suleiman looked confused regarding what to do next. Harry was cool, even amused, realizing that they had fallen into his trap and had started to believe what he was saying. He responded to Suleiman, saying that his boss at Palkhivala & Palkhivala suspected that someone in their office was passing on information to the ex-maharaja for a hefty fee. It was likely that this person had given this incorrect information to the ex-maharaja's team to justify the fee he was getting. He realized it was also likely the reason why they had lost the earlier case before the Rajasthan High Court. Harry said that he did not have the certificate but now knew for sure that there was a spy in the office. Someone was passing information to the opponents.

Suleiman was now convinced that Harry was speaking the truth. The story of Harry obtaining the certificate could well have been a fabrication by their mole in the Palkhivala & Palkhivala office to extricate even more money from the ex-maharaja.

However, it was still a victory of sorts for the ex-maharaja. In the absence of any evidence, the case was as good as over. Despite a very thorough search of Harry's person and belongings, nothing had been found. Harry overheard one of the junior customs officers called Awasthy whispering to his senior that the young lawyer from Britain was clean and that they may have crossed a line by hitting him and frisking him based on hearsay. He seemed like an ethical man, and Harry zeroed in on him for help in eventually retrieving the certificate from the washroom.

After three hours of grilling, Harry was allowed to walk out. As he walked out of the customs office, Suleiman smugly remarked that he was satisfied that Harry did not have the certificate. Maharaja Karan Singh would lose the case in its absence. Suleiman had a look of triumph on his face.

Harry did not tell anyone in his office about the certificate he had hidden in the washroom of Palam Airport, lest the information was misused. He waited for a week and just two days before the case was listed for hearing in the Supreme Court of India, he approached Awasthy and invited him to a restaurant in Connaught Place. He was taking a chance in trusting Awasthy, but he had a gut feeling that he was doing the right thing.

As they sat down to sip coffee, Harry explained how he had suspected foul play upon seeing saw four customs officials coming towards him, and how he had hidden the certificate in a sealed plastic bag behind the cistern in the washroom. Harry's hunch was right. Awasthy was an upright officer and had vowed to work with honesty in a department notorious for its corruption. He agreed to help Harry and the next evening, he met Harry again at the same restaurant and smoothly handed over the certificate to him. No one came to know of the meeting. The customs officer even paid the bill of the restaurant.

The case was listed before the division bench of the Supreme

Court, and the courtroom was jammed with lawyers, petitioners and the media. Ranbir Singh was also present, a satisfied expression on his face, expecting to walk away with a verdict that would put millions in his pocket.

As Mr Rustom Palkhivala got up to argue the case, Harry walked up to him and produced the missing certificate placing it as part of the exhibit. Ranbir Singh's jaw dropped. There was nothing he could do. He realized in that minute that he had turned into a pauper.

Every property that the self-serving and unethical ex-maharaja had quickly seized, based on the high court order, was wrested back by the apex court and handed to the family of his younger brother. The ex-maharaja was once again forced to abdicate his assets to Maharaja Karan Singh. The ordinance certificate, now lying on the table as Exhibit No. 47, was proof of the abdication of his throne as well his assets in favour of his younger brother.

The case was covered in every newspaper. The law firm promoted Harry to become a partner, an honour that was quite unprecedented for someone so young. But more than the promotion, Harry was content with the personal victory, though he didn't speak about it with anyone, that he had been able to partly avenge his father's murder.

Now, he had one more petition to file—to reopen the famous Raisina Hall murder case and bring the real perpetrator behind those multiple crimes on a cold January night in 1941, former Maharaja Ranbir Singh, to justice.

He shared the blow-by-blow account of the entire court proceedings with his mother—how the ordinance was produced, the restoration of justice to Maharaja Karan Singh, and the shocked expression on Ranbir Singh's face. They sat together on the spacious lawn of her new bungalow in Greater Kailash as he told her how it all unfolded. She felt satisfied that, at long last, justice had been done—that the cruel Ranbir Singh, who had first used her and then destroyed her life by killing her beloved Javed, would finally face the heat of the court. She closed her eyes and sent a prayer of gratitude to the Almighty for her son's return and for his loving care. She kissed him softly on the forehead. Then she suggested that he meet a distant cousin's daughter, Ayesha, for a marriage alliance. At first, Harry refused but then agreed to meet Ayesha. Perhaps they would marry, Fatima hoped, and perhaps they would settle down in New Delhi. Her long-lost son may, at last, be restored to her.

Before leaving for Paris, a depressed Ranbir Singh expressed a desire to meet Harry. He wanted to know why a British lawyer had specially flown down to India and taken so much trouble to nail him. Harry agreed to meet him in the lobby of the Imperial Hotel where the ex-maharaja was staying. As Ranbir Singh came down the stairs, something about Harry's face stopped him in his tracks. He seemed familiar and yet couldn't put his finger on it. Harry then gave him two pieces of news that cut the ground from under the former maharaja's feet.

One was that he had been able to obtain a subpoena from the district courts for Ranbir Singh's involvement in the gruesome murder of Javed Khan and Pratap Singh Rajput on the night of 30 January 1941 on Raisina Hill, and also for the murder of the cousin. Ranbir Singh would now be facing a murder charge under Section 302 and Section 120B of the Indian Penal Code and most likely would spend the rest of his life in prison.

Secondly, he told Ranbir Singh that his real name was Javed Khan and that he was the son of Fatima Begum and the man she had loved, his former aide Javed Khan. After giving Ranbir Singh this information, he got up, turned around, and walked out of the lobby. Just before he left, he turned around one last time to see the expression on Ranbir Singh's shocked face, now completely drained of all colour.

That same night, the former maharaja suffered a stroke and before morning, he was dead. As it turned out, and in the way destiny sometimes plays its hand, the date was 30 January 1966, exactly twenty-five years after the attack at Raisina Hill.

SEVEN

HYDERABAD HORROR

Part I

The sun was beginning to set on the dusty village of Sumali, located near Unnao in Uttar Pradesh. The village was like many other small villages of India—insignificant and unremarkable.

It was in this village that Dinu and Pali first met at the age of five in the government primary school. They became friends and were eventually inseparable. The fact that they were from different religions did not get in the way of their friendship. They spent all their time together. They shared their food, joys and sorrows. They were there for each other through good times and bad. Their real names were Fakkrudin and Devender Pal, but everyone knew them only as Dinu and Pali. Although they both came from poor families and were completely uninterested in their studies, they shared a love for the good life. They were determined to somehow become rich and successful.

Most of the inhabitants of this tiny village earned their livelihood by working in a brick kiln. Both Dinu's and Pali's fathers worked in the factory as daily wage labourers. The only other source of employment was agriculture. Most people in the area lived below the poverty line. The flat-roofed huts did not have electricity nor were there any streetlights. The village was plunged into an ominous darkness as soon as the sun went down. So, the villagers had to make do with lanterns.

Even with the state they were in, Dinu's mother was a caring woman who loved her four children. Dinu, the youngest, was pampered the most by his mother. She tried to tolerate her alcoholic and emotionally distant husband. He never talked to her about the children's future. But, to his credit, he never misbehaved with the children. Still, he was a detached and inattentive father.

Pali's mother had been embittered by the challenges life had thrown at her. She complained constantly, filling the air with her rants. She argued endlessly with her husband over his drinking habit. She was subjected to domestic violence. Life in the household went round and round in the same circle. Almost every evening, the children witnessed heated arguments, which culminated in their drunken father beating their mother black and blue.

One evening, as the last crimson rays of the sun disappeared behind the Sumali hillock, Pali returned home after playing in the fields with his friends and asked his mother for food. It was seven in the evening. As usual, he seemed to have stepped into the middle of a fight. 'What did I do to be married to this useless drunkard? Why is my luck so rotten?' his mother was screaming. She turned towards Pali and continued her tirade, 'This man spends all day smoking his hookah and drinking alcohol. He has no qualms, no scruples. He would rather buy a bottle of country liquor for twenty-six rupees than bring home any ration so I can make food for all of you...' She was suddenly interrupted by a hard slap on the face. She was so busy lambasting her husband that she did not notice him charge at her.

'You bitch! You good-for-nothing woman! One day, I will kill you. Don't you dare open your mouth when I am drinking. Don't you dare get in the way,' he yelled, raising his hand to strike again.

This time, Pali's mother dodged him and hurled some more abuses at him. She was not one to take anything lying down. Nor was Pali's father, once provoked, easy to stop. His language got filthier as he continued to abuse his wife and all her relatives. Pali felt like he did not exist, as if neither of his parents could see him.

This was a familiar scene in Pali's home, and he knew that there would be no dinner tonight. He ran to Dinu's house, hoping that he would get something to eat there. Dinu's mother had a generous heart and shared whatever food was available, despite a scarcity of resources.

Life went on in much the same way. Pali went frequently to Dinu's home for food as the tensions between his parents escalated, and he became virtually invisible in his own home.

Dinu and Pali were eleven years old when they decided to skip school and spend the day at the Diwali fete being held on the outskirts of the village. They spent the entire day at the fete, and by evening, they were famished. Since neither had any money, they decided to steal some food from a stall. Dinu kept the stall keeper engrossed by asking the prices of different items while Pali stealthily stole some food items. Pali ran away and was later joined by Dinu. This was the first time they had done this, and since they got away easily, they developed the confidence to steal stuff from the other stalls.

Pali stole some bangles and an artificial necklace from a stall. No one saw them. In the evening, Pali presented the jewellery to his mother. Instead of scolding him for stealing, she hugged him. She was delighted with the gift. It had been a long time since she had embraced her son. The boys were encouraged by this gesture and decided to return to the fete and steal whatever they could lay their hands on.

The next day, Dinu brazenly grabbed some notes from the

cash box of a stall keeper. No one noticed or raised the alarm. Either luck was with them or they were smart enough to not get caught. This was fun, and it felt great to finally have some cash in their pockets.

Over the next few months, they were emboldened further and became petty thieves or what was called *chindi chor* in common parlance. They stole small items here and there, and since no shopkeeper in the village maintained a stock inventory, the theft went undetected. Next, they set their sights on Unnao, which was situated near the industrial town of Kanpur and was fast developing into a manufacturing hub. Many businessmen were shifting their factories to Unnao, where land was much cheaper than Kanpur. The growing prosperity of Unnao offered Dinu and Pali many opportunities to practise their newfound skills.

By the time they were fifteen, Dinu and Pali had become full-fledged, knife-wielding thieves. Both had given up their studies and were encouraged by Pali's mother to steal and buy her gifts. They became more and more audacious, taking greater risks but somehow never getting caught.

Before long, they were making regular trips to Kanpur, where there was more wealth and more items to steal. Beginning from chain-snatching and minor break-ins, they ventured to steal items from fancy showrooms. They had become seasoned thieves with the audacity that came from never getting caught.

With each theft, their ambition and the lust for a good life increased. They stole brazenly and spent the money on nightclubs and fancy restaurants. They always kept some money aside for Pali's mother, who made delicacies each time they handed her an expensive gift. She never reprimanded or discouraged them from stealing. It was her tacit acceptance, and even appreciation, of the material goods they were bringing into her life that motivated them to steal again and again. One time, when Pali gifted her some stolen sarees, she made the special cookies that he loved and pampered him as if he had done the greatest thing ever.

Apart from Pali's mother, no one had a clue to what the boys were up to. Neither of the boys had studied beyond the sixth standard, but they now had more money than they had ever seen before.

They stashed their booty, which included several gold bangles and some cash, in an old dilapidated structure just outside their village. The abandoned house was believed to be haunted, which kept people away, making it a perfect place for hiding valuables. Pali and Dinu had no regrets about the life they had chosen. Their philosophy was: money is good, and the more the better. They were also not afraid of the stories circulated about the haunted house.

By the time they were seventeen, the two boys had raging hormones. Their curiosity about sex grew. One time, Dinu noticed a village girl going early in the morning to the fields to answer the call of nature. He found his eyes following her; his desire was aroused. He called Pali, and they both decided to have a look at her and molest her the next morning.

The next morning, they crept stealthily towards her and grabbed her. They were hidden in the tall grass of the fields. While Dinu held her hands and kept a cloth on her mouth to prevent her from screaming, Pali raped her. Then it was Dinu's turn to quench his thirst, with Pali giving him a helping hand. Once they had finished, the girl managed to wriggle out of their grip and run towards the village.

Again, no one got to know what they had done because the poor girl was too terrified to tell anyone of her ordeal. Dinu and Pali laughed at how easily they always managed to get away with things, especially things that seemed risky but which always turned out to be easy for them.

They had never been caught. It was almost as if Providence was helping them, even encouraging them; they felt justified in all the things they did. After thefts, they had committed a heinous crime like rape. Still, they were roaming freely. Dinu and Pali felt invincible. They were convinced they could do anything and get away with it.

Both had taken jobs at a vehicle mechanic's garage in Unnao where they learned how to drive as well as how to repair trucks. Unknown to the garage owner, they often took out one of the vehicles in the garage to commit petty crimes at night. They had left their homes in the small village where they grew up. Neither of them had any respect or love for their parents or siblings. They believed they were meant for bigger things. They slept in the garage and their 'escapades' at night pleased them no end.

By the time they were nineteen, Dinu and Pali were hardened criminals with no regrets and no remorse. They were no longer *chindi chors* (petty thieves). Even Unnao was too small for them now.

Certain developments compelled them to leave Unnao by train and head for Bhopal, where, thanks to their ability to drive and repair trucks, they got a job with a local transporter. Dinu drove the truck back and forth from Bhopal to Bangalore, while Pali worked as a cleaner. They also had two assistants who would help load and unload the goods that were being transported.

Gradually, the two helpers were roped to help in the crimes. The four would remove a small portion of the goods they were transporting, sell them, and keep the money. They replaced the original items with fake ones so that the quantity delivered to the customers remained the same.

Eventually, complaints started pouring in from customers. Dinu and Pali were reprimanded by their employer. This did not deter them, it only made them smarter. They began to now surreptitiously steal goods from other cargo-laden trucks parked on the outskirts of the city to pay octroi. On the few occasions that they did get caught, they were smart enough to bribe the police officers on duty and get away.

Dinu and Pali were fully criminalized; they stole whenever they saw the opportunity. Money fattened their pockets. They had also got into the habit of drinking and taking drugs.

As winter set in, Dinu, Pali and their two accomplices were entrusted with the task of picking up sponge iron and iron ingots from Uttar Pradesh. The consignment had to be delivered to Hyderabad. It was to be a long drive back and forth. On 21 December, they loaded the truck with the ingots and left Uttar Pradesh for the three-day journey to Hyderabad to deliver the consignment.

Always on the lookout for how they could make money for themselves, Dinu and Pali had decided to illegally carry an extra load of steel channels from Bhopal to Hyderabad and sell them to an acquaintance who would give them seven thousand rupees in exchange. They planned to spend this money on a brothel they had frequented before, located near Mahbubnagar in Hyderabad.

They reached Hyderabad on 24 December, three days after they left Bhopal. They first unloaded the illegal booty and pocketed the money promised by their acquaintance. They then headed to their final destination to offload the rest of the ingots. They were happy. They had money in their pockets, and the drive was spent laughing and fantasizing about the fun they would have at the Mahbubnagar brothel that night. They were full of lust.

Just as they were driving into Mahbubnagar, a joint team of the Regional Transport Authority and Enforcement Department intercepted them. Dinu did not have a valid licence. His ability to get away with things had made him overconfident. He had not bothered to renew the licence for two years. The four were asked to step down from the truck and show their identity cards. Only

Pali had a voter card, none of the others had any valid form of identification at all. The officials decided to impound the vehicle and take it to the nearest police station.

Good at wriggling out of tricky situations, Pali took out the seven thousand rupees in his pocket and offered it as a bribe to the officials. It didn't work. Dinu cunningly removed the self-start cable to prevent the truck from moving. Exasperated, the officials imposed a penalty of six thousand rupees, issued a receipt, and warned the four men to carry proper identification or their vehicle would be impounded the next time. The four folded their hands before the government officials but were full of glee inside. They had got away yet again.

Though they had cleverly escaped harassment by the authorities, they now had only a thousand rupees left—not enough to go to the brothel and have the night they had planned. All they could afford now were some snacks and some hard liquor, after which they would have to make the long journey back to Bhopal. Dinu fixed the self-start cable back in the truck, but it moved only about 100 yards before it sputtered to a stop just outside Civil Hospital. It wouldn't restart.

Part II

Inside the hospital, Dr Mrinal Mukherji was busy assisting senior cardiologist and heart surgeon Dr Reddy in an open-heart surgery. Despite being fairly young, in the short span of two years, Dr Mrinal had achieved enough expertise to do heart surgeries and sustain the heart during the procedure. In the old days, the heart was removed, kept in a frozen environment during the operation, and then revived back into beating using electric shocks. The success rate was barely 50 per cent back then. Now, due to medical advancements, open-heart surgeries were performed while the patient's heart continued to function enough to pump blood to all parts of the body.

Dr Reddy was a widely recognized name in the field of open-heart surgery. He had come to rely more and more on the meticulous support that his young medical assistant Dr Mrinal gave him. As she assisted her superior, Dr Mrinal had no clue what lay ahead of her that night.

The surgery was complicated and had taken well over four hours. It was 11.30 p.m. By the time, she washed her hands and changed her clothes, it was past midnight. Her friend Madhu, a resident doctor at the hospital, suggested that it was late and she should stay the night in her room. But Dr Mrinal assured her that she often rode back at odd hours from the hospital on her scooter and that she would be perfectly safe.

Moreover, despite her friend's sensible advice, Dr Mrinal was eager to go home because it was her parents' fortieth wedding anniversary the next day and she had taken the day off to be with them. She was their only child and was looking forward to celebrating with them as soon as they woke up.

Mrinal was born eleven years after her parents' marriage. Desperate for a child, they had tried everything—from medicines to hakims to praying to Goddess Kali at Durga Puja. Mrinal's father, Ram Mukherji, had wanted to become a doctor himself. He could not realize that dream because of financial difficulties. When his daughter was born, he was determined to somehow find a way to make his only child a doctor. At that time, he worked as a compounder in Kolkata with a renowned doctor, Dr Jaggan Rao. As he watched the doctor work, he yearned for his daughter to join the medical profession.

After his wife passed away, Dr Rao decided to move out of Kolkata and shift his practice to Hyderabad, where his two daughters lived. Both were married to Sindhi brothers living at Babukhan Road in Hyderabad. Both the brothers worked in a jewellery showroom by the name of Meena Jewellers.

Ram too decided to shift to Hyderabad along with his employer and mentor. There, Dr Rao re-established his practice. He was a pious and kind-hearted man who offered to pay the entire fee for Mrinal's MBBS education. He was also instrumental in getting her an internship at Civil Hospital. The day the vivacious Mrinal became a qualified doctor, the Mukherjis invited the entire neighbourhood for dinner and profusely thanked Dr Rao for his generosity.

They had been living in Hyderabad for the past nine years. After completing her internship, Mrinal got a job as a junior doctor at Civil Hospital, thanks again to Dr Rao's recommendation. When she received her first salary, it was a momentous day for the family. She presented her entire salary of fourteen thousand rupees to her mother. She also selected a special golf cap for Dr Rao, who was an avid golf player. Her father, who had started as Dr Rao's compounder, was ecstatic at his daughter's accomplishment. His daughter was a doctor. His dream came true for his daughter, and what he could not achieve himself, he did through his daughter.

Dr Mrinal continued to do well. Her courage and zeal helped her excel at her work. Dr Reddy, the senior cardiologist at the hospital, saw a spark in the young doctor. Impressed at her hard work and devotion, he offered her a position as his first assistant.

Dr Mrinal was trusted with greater responsibilities. Within a few months, she had saved enough money to buy herself a scooter. This would make her independent and save a lot of the time she spent waiting for buses. Moreover, instead of walking, she could now ride her scooter to the local government school where she frequently gave lectures on health and hygiene, which were attended by many people in the neighbourhood.

Life was good for Mrinal. Her reputation as an excellent doctor was growing. Thanks to her handy scooter, she could now easily go to places and live a happy and full life. She had just celebrated her twenty-eighth birthday a few days ago and her parents had coaxed her into accepting the marriage proposal of a nice, gentle Bengali boy who also lived in Hyderabad.

She didn't know then that the same scooter which had brought her so much freedom would change her life in a cruel twist of fate.

Part III

That fateful day when Dr Mrinal stepped out of the hospital at midnight, the roads were deserted. She got onto her scooter and began driving home, tired but satisfied at how well the very complex surgery had gone. She was crossing Shamsabad Road when her scooter suddenly jerked and the rear tire's tube burst. She got down to see what had happened only to realize that she had a flat tire. How to handle this at such a late hour?

She looked around for help but there was nobody around. It was dark and she was alone. Only a truck was parked nearby. About a hundred-and-fifty feet away, a petrol pump seemed to be functioning, and she decided to walk there and try and get some help.

Pali noticed the young woman, who seemed to be in distress,

walking alone down the road. Quite drunk by now, he got down from the truck and walked up to her. He said he was a mechanic and could change the tire for her. Dr Mrinal thanked him but became a little nervous when she saw two more men come over. She had not noticed Dinu and one of the helpers walking toward her in the semi-darkness.

The tire was replaced but Dr Mrinal could sense the tension in the air. She put on a bold face and, after thanking Pali, was about to kick-start the scooter when Dinu grabbed her arm. Pali quickly covered her mouth with his hand to prevent her from screaming. The helper lifted her off her feet and the three of them took her to the truck parked nearby.

Mrinal flailed around struggling to free herself, but the three men were all drunk and much too strong for her. They pinned her down now on the empty floor of the truck. She tried to shout for help but no voice came out. Her body and brain were frozen in shock. She wasn't able to move, think or cry for help.

Dinu got behind the steering wheel and drove the truck to a nearby secluded area and then they dragged her into a field with tall grass and bushes. They were well hidden. She again tried to scream and free herself, but the sex-starved foursome would not let her go. Not till they had satisfied their lust.

The helper brought a bottle of liquor from inside the truck and Pali forced it into her mouth. Mrinal tried to scream again. This time, he tore off a piece of her shirt and stuffed it into her mouth. Dinu hit her hard across her face and told her to shut up. The nightmare wouldn't end. She was hysterical and in agony. The four men became violent, hitting her and pinching her private parts. No one came to her help.

One by one, the four men forced themselves on her, raping her in turn. By now, she had lost consciousness and had no idea how many times the men had assaulted her. When she regained consciousness, she realized that the men had exhausted themselves.

She again tried to wriggle out and finally managed to let out a scream. As one of the labourers tried to muzzle her, she kicked him with her leg. In a fit of rage, Pali picked up a stone and hit her on the head, cracking her skull open. A stream of blood spurted out and within a few minutes, Dr Mrinal was dead.

Pali saw the frozen expression on her face and realized he had killed her. The life had gone out of her face but her eyes continued to stare at him. That look on her face went through him like a shock wave and for a few moments, there was pin-drop silence. Then the panic set in and the men decided to dump the body where it was and run away immediately toward Bhopal. But Pali said that it would be better to burn the body. He remembered he had done the same thing outside Kanpur once, and no one had ever managed to trace the criminal act. They should do the same thing again.

Pali asked Dinu to drive the truck towards the lone petrol pump at Shamsabad Road. They needed at least three or four litres of petrol to burn the body fully. They did not want to leave any traces of the girl or the crime committed by them.

Pali got down from the truck and walked with a five-litre can to the petrol pump. The attendant at the pump was fast asleep. Pali woke him up and told him that he needed petrol since his vehicle was stranded five kilometres away in Mahbubnagar. The attendant was a little surprised since there were at least three petrol pumps on the way which were much closer. Nevertheless, he filled the can with petrol and took the money from Pali.

Soon after, Dinu also drove up to the petrol pump in the truck and asked the attendant to fill it up. They had searched Dr Mrinal's pockets and found two thousand and three hundred rupees. After the truck was filled up, he turned around and headed back. On the way, he picked up Pali, who was walking toward the body with the petrol can in his hand.

By this time, the two helpers, Shyam and Rupam were breaking down. Both were jittery and shaking with fear. In a fit of lust, they had become party to a crime that was way beyond stealing some iron ingots or steel pipes. Dinu tried to calm them down. 'Relax, both of you,' he said. 'We'll soon burn the body and nobody will recognize her. We've done this before and no one ever found out. Don't worry, we'll be fine.' He winked at Pali, who did not utter a word. He had murdered a young woman. The look in her eyes, staring straight at him, sent a chill down his spine.

Dinu continued, 'I searched her pockets and found two thousand and three hundred rupees, and I also took her watch. We will easily get five thousand rupees for this. She won't need it now.' He let out a malicious chuckle, alcohol still on his breath. 'Relax, folks. We will be far, far away from Hyderabad before anyone discovers this. We've never been caught. The world is full of fools, you only need to be smart enough to fool them.'

The four poured petrol on Dr Mrinal's body and set it on fire. Within minutes, the body began burning down. Seeing that the body was mostly burnt, they got into the truck and headed back towards Bhopal. As they crossed the octroi, it began to rain. None of them said a single word during the entire journey back to Bhopal.

The next morning, some passers-by noticed a half-burnt body in the fields and reported it to the police. The police station was nine hundred feet away from the spot where the crime had been committed. Soon, police officers turned up at the spot and examined the body. The news of a body found in the fields spread like wildfire.

The police investigations and the autopsy report revealed that the woman's body had been dragged to an empty field near the Honda Toll II Plaza in the Shamsabad area, and that she had been raped multiple times. The investigation also suggested that she was probably smothered while being raped to prevent her screams from being heard.

Meanwhile, Dr Mrinal's parents woke up with a growing sense of anxiety. Their daughter had not returned home the night before. They called the hospital only to be told that she had not stayed overnight there and had left for her home around midnight on her scooter. They rushed to the hospital and found no sign of her. No one had seen her since last night. Sensing something amiss, the hospital authorities informed the police about the missing doctor.

On their fortieth wedding anniversary, Dr Mrinal's parents received news that terrified them. A burnt body had been found in a field near the toll plaza. A scooter was parked about one kilometre away. Dr Mrinal's mother fainted on hearing the news. Her husband broke down. Although they did not know for sure, they had an ominous feeling that the body may be that of their only child.

The police lodged an FIR regarding a missing person, and with a trembling hand, Dr Mrinal's father signed it. The media was all over the place by now. Sensational reports were being flashed across television channels. Reporters were interviewing the hospital staff and others in the neighbourhood. The director-general of the Hyderabad police immediately knew this was going to be a sensitive case. He summoned his most diligent and upright officer Superintendent of Police (SP) Ravi Raj, who had solved more cases than any other officer, to take charge of the case.

The smart officer wasted no time. He knew this case would attract wide publicity and he quickly ordered an autopsy and forensic examination of the body. There was no clue or identification document found on or near the body. It was very likely that they had burnt them along with the victim. He went around searching for any vehicle nearby and was able to locate the abandoned scooter a kilometre away. Though some identity documents were found on the scooter, they still had to be verified and linked with the victim.

Next, Ravi ordered his team to locate all CCTV cameras installed within a one-kilometre range and to check with all the local police stations about missing persons. One of his subordinates came back with the information that Mr Mukherji had complained to the town police station about his missing 28-year-old daughter Dr Mrinal Mukherji. The name matched the documents found on the scooter.

Ravi went through all the CCTV footage minute by minute. It revealed Dr Mrinal going on her scooter towards town. Another CCTV camera footage showed the attendant at the petrol pump selling petrol in a can to a buyer who seemed nervous and overcautious. Ravi set aside the footage and did not reveal his investigation strategy to anyone, even his subordinates.

He spent two days in intense investigation himself. He found further clues in the CCTV footage installed at the petrol pump and in the statement of the attendant at the petrol pump. The attendant confirmed that he had indeed sold five litres of petrol to a man in the middle of the night, that the man had seemed nervous and agitated, and strangely, the man had walked five kilometres to this petrol pump when there were other petrol pumps between Mahbubnagar and Shamsabad. Moreover, the dialect of the man who bought the petrol was different from the dialect spoken in Hyderabad. His dialect suggested he came from Uttar Pradesh. Something was not right.

Dr Mrinal's parents received the shocking and sad confirmation of their daughter's death on the evening of their fortieth wedding anniversary. Their daughter was twenty-eight years old. She had been a brilliant student. She had excelled at work. She was to be married to a good-looking Bengali boy in Kolkata in a few months. No one could have foreseen the tragic way her life would end. For that matter, no one could imagine the impact her death would have on the entire country.

The case began to hit national headlines and the brutal crime drew widespread condemnation. It seemed to be the only thing people spoke of. Politicians began to drop in to the Mukherji's residence to pay their condolences and some even gave press interviews expressing their revulsion to such terrible, unprovoked violence. 'What those men did to the innocent doctor is another reminder of how unsafe we have allowed our society to become by not ensuring swift and firm justice in such cases,' tweeted a famous film personality.

Another actor gave a television interview. He said it was high time the nation woke up and instilled fear in the minds of criminals so that no one would even dare to think of committing such a horrific crime. He termed it the 'Hyderbad Horror'. The phrase went viral and people all over the country began to refer to Dr Mrinal's case as the Hyderabad Horror.

The pressure was on for the police and within a week, Ravi Raj delivered the criminals. In bold headlines, the morning papers claimed that two truck drivers named Dinu and Pali and their two helpers had been arrested for the rape and murder of the young doctor in Shamsabad.

Ravi Raj was mobbed by the press for details. At a jam-packed press conference, he revealed the story of how the crime unfolded. Truck drivers Dinu and Pali, both twenty-six years old, and their two helpers aged twenty-three and twenty-one, had seen Dr Mrinal struggling with her punctured scooter near their truck in the middle of the night. Pali had approached the doctor on the pretext of helping her and then suddenly, the other three accused had pounced on her from the darkness and dragged her towards a nearby field. There, each of them had repeatedly raped her. When she had tried to scream for help, Pali had smothered her and hit her over the head when she tried to escape, which led to her death. He had then walked to the more distant petrol pump, rather than the ones close by to avoid linking them with the crime. He brought the petrol back in a can and the four then set her body on fire.

The government set up a fast-track court on the chief minister's instructions to expeditiously deal with the gruesome murder and to bring stringent punishment to the perpetrators of the crime. Ravi got written statements from all the four accused under Section 164 of the Criminal Procedure Code.

Dr Mrinal's parents were bombarded by visitors, both press and politicians, wanting to express sympathy. They requested that they be left alone to grieve privately for their daughter. They only wanted a speedy trial and justice.

A controversy of sorts erupted when one of the ministers was quoted saying that the crime was the victim's fault. Girls should not move around on deserted roads after nine o'clock at night. His comments were widely condemned by the media and the public. Social media went wild condemning his regressive comments.

Even though in jail, Pali remained cocky. In one of his statements, he confessed to having committed at least ten other rapes in and around Unnao and Kanpur. He boasted that they had never been caught as no one ever complained and that the village women they raped seemed to tolerate the attacks for reasons unknown.

After being mercilessly beaten by the police, Pali admitted to burning one of his rape victims on the outskirts of Kanpur three years ago. This was a rape and murder case that the police had closely investigated at that time but due to the lack of evidence, had had to close the file.

Ravi recorded Dinu's statements about similar criminal activities going back several years. More details of their modus operandi emerged. One of Dinu's statements, recorded under Section 164 of the Criminal Procedure Code, went thus:

> We have been committing all kinds of thefts for years. The police never caught us. We were smarter than others. We both lived a dual life. In the day, we worked as mechanics in a garage in Unnao. At night, we roamed the wealthier parts of Kanpur such as Swaroop Nagar, Aaya Nagar and Moti Jheel looking for what we could easily steal. We took stereos from cars parked outside and removed tires along with their rims and sold them to an acquaintance in Chor Bazaar.
>
> Once, while prowling at night, we saw a woman walking alone. She looked like she belonged to a wealthy family. It was late and the streets were deserted. We followed her into the shadows and pounced on her to rob her. Pali inserted a cloth into her mouth and I pulled off her expensive jewellery. She looked terrified and tried to call out for help when Pali hit her with a wrench he was carrying with him. She fell and lost consciousness.
>
> We decided to take maximum advantage of the situation and raped her repeatedly. When she regained consciousness, she abused us in filthy language and said our days were numbered. She said she was the real sister of the most dreaded gangster of Kanpur, Don Baldev Rana. She cursed us and said he would finish us off.
>
> On hearing this, instead of running away, we decided

to kill her to protect ourselves. We choked her and threw her body in a nearby drain. It rained heavily that night and she was swept away in the water. We were never caught.

We returned to Unnao and decided to quit our jobs at the garage. We travelled aimlessly toward Jhansi, Khajuraho and then eventually got a job with the transporter in Bhopal.

Luck favoured us again since a rumour had quickly spread in Kanpur that Baldev Rana's sister was killed by his rival Ranvijay Singh, who controlled the unions of the industrial town.

Instead of looking for us, Baldev Rana, aided surreptitiously by the police, went on a rampage against Ranvijay Singh and his henchmen. Later, we got to know that he had taken revenge and wiped out Ranvijay Singh's entire gang. We laughed. We got away again. We truly believed nothing could touch us.

An informer told us that the police themselves had a big hand in spreading the rumour that Baldev Rana's sister was killed at the behest of Ranvijay Singh. They knew what Baldev's reaction would be and an entire criminal gang would be wiped out.

It so happened that a sub-inspector in Hyderabad was earlier posted in Kanpur and had been on the payroll of Baldev Rana. He clandestinely gave a copy of Dinu's confession statement to Baldev Rana for which he was handsomely rewarded. Rana now set his eyes on finding the real criminals who had raped and killed his sister: Dinu and Pali. He was waiting for an opportunity to kill them both, and that opportunity came when the duo was brought to Unnao District Court to be tried for their offenses.

Dinu and Pali were taken under heavy police custody to the courtroom to be tried before the chief judicial magistrate of Unnao. While the court proceedings were going on, three assailants led by Baldev Rana stormed into the courtroom and began firing indiscriminately at Dinu and Pali. A bullet hit a police constable who died on the spot. Also present were special personnel of the Uttar Pradesh police and a team of seven police officers from Hyderabad. As the bullets rang out, there was utter mayhem.

Some of the police officials sustained bullet injuries. Both the accused ducked and managed to escape getting hit. Two constables had the presence of mind to quickly cordon off the courtroom by locking the gates. Meanwhile, the chief judicial magistrate rushed to his chamber after one bullet missed him narrowly.

There was a heavy exchange of fire in which Baldev Rana and three policemen died in the courtroom. The other two assailants were arrested. People were screaming everywhere. Taking advantage of the chaos, Dinu and Pali escaped from the courtroom. The revenge killing by Baldev Rana for his sister's rape and murder killed a lot of people. But Dinu and Pali had got away—yet again.

The police launched a nationwide hunt for the two criminals. There was outrage over the incident. Both houses of Parliament were in a furore. The MPs called for stringent measures to catch and punish the absconders. Castration was suggested. Several celebrities spoke up and demanded harsh and immediate punishment for the offenders. Television channels were full of minute-by-minute reporting of the happenings. The brutal rape and murder of the doctor had already sent shockwaves across the country. As other crimes committed by Dinu and Pali were revealed, there was complete outrage. How could such a daring daylight escape be possible right under the noses of the large army of policemen on site? A judicial inquiry was ordered and police teams were packed off to Kanpur, Bhopal, and even Mumbai and Delhi. But no information or clue was found on the missing criminals. They were gone.

Dinu and Pali had hidden in the dilapidated structure on

the outskirts of their village Sumali, the same place where they stored their weapons and stolen goods when they first took to a life of crime. At that time, they were petty thieves. Now they had returned as rapists and murderers. They knew that if they were caught, they would either be hanged to death or if a mercy petition was accepted either by the Supreme Court or by the President of India, then they would get life imprisonment, but nothing less. The end was near. Either the police would get them. Or, Baldev Rana's gang would.

For three days, they survived on water from the river nearby and whatever fruits they could find in the forest area around Unnao. But by the fourth day, hunger won over fear and they came out of hiding to search for food. They were starving and tried to steal food from the first roadside *dhaba* (eatery) they came across. The owner of the dhaba, a burly Sikh, caught them red-handed and thrashed them. They begged to be released, but he summoned the police instead and handed them over.

Before getting caught by the dhaba owner, Dinu had managed to stuff his pockets with notes stolen from the cash box kept next to the tandoor. He offered them to the police sub-inspector as they were being driven to the police station. The inspector refused and ordered his subordinate to lodge an FIR against them for theft. At the police station, he asked the head constable to do a full-body search for any other currency notes or weapons that they might have on them.

No one at the police station recognized that the two most-wanted criminals in India were right here, under their noses and in their custody. Perhaps they would get away with a small rap on their knuckles.

That is when their luck ran out. A constable, who had been released from Civil Hospital after being wounded in the Unnao court carnage, had come to deliver some documents to the station house officer. He recognized Dinu and Pali immediately. Police officials all over the country were hunting for these men and had been unable to find them. And here they were, the two men accused of committing the most brutal crime ever seen in Hyderabad and Kanpur.

The news spread like lightning. Within minutes, the police station was swarming with cameramen and reporters. High-ranking police officers and politicians also crowded the station. Breaking news reports began to flash across all television channels: the offenders who had escaped from a packed courtroom had been recaptured. The police downplayed the fact that the capture happened by chance because of a roadside dhaba owner and instead took all the credit for the arrest of the high-profile criminals. The DIG of Unnao gave interviews on his elaborate planning that had led to the arrest of the two men.

The next morning, the recapture of the criminals was the lead story in every newspaper. Photographs of Dinu and Pali in handcuffs were splashed across the front page. On hearing the news, Pali's mother and father came to meet him at the police station, and only after much pleading were they allowed to see their son. Dinu's parents did not even bother to meet their son who had left them several years ago.

Pali met his mother amid heavy police presence. His weeping mother stretched her arms to meet him, but Pali came close and bit her ear lobe with his teeth. She cried out in shock and pain. She was bewildered at Pali's action. Pali told her that he would have cut off her tongue with his knife if he had not been handcuffed. His words were laced with bitterness. He shouted at her and said that had she only discouraged him from stealing money and other items during his school days, he may never have taken to a life of crime. Instead, she not only encouraged him but took delight in all the gifts he brought her with stolen money. That encouragement, he accused her, had made him what he was today: India's most wanted criminal.

Police personnel came to his mother's rescue as Pali spat his venom on her, and both Dinu and Pali were put in solitary confinement before being taken away by flight from Kanpur to Hyderabad, amidst hundreds of bulbs flashing all over. This time, the police were taking no chances. The police force had been widely blamed for letting the hardened criminals escape the first time, despite several policemen present in court. Now they had Dinu and Pali in chains from neck to feet. There was no way they could escape again.

The four accused had already admitted before a magistrate how they had forcibly abducted the doctor when she was seeking help with her scooter. They had pretended to help her and then taken her to the fields and brutally raped her before finally burning her dead body.

⚜

Part IV

Three days later, the newspapers reported a sensational development. All the four accused in the kidnap, rape and murder of Dr Mrinal were killed in an encounter early Sunday morning when they tried to escape. The encounter happened near Shadnagar, where they had committed the crime.

The SP in charge alleged that the four had been taken to the crime scene to 'reconstruct' the crime as part of the inquiry and preparation of the charge-sheet. He said that one of the accused had snatched the revolver from a police officer present and had opened fire on them. The other three had picked up stones and rocks and tried to injure the rest and then tried to flee in the darkness. The twelve police officials present had to fire back. All four accused had been killed—in the same spot where they had committed the crime.

Dr Mrinal's parents, heartbroken at the loss of their daughter, were relieved that justice had been served. Thousands of Hyderabad residents congregated on the crime spot and shouted slogans praising the encounter.

The SP confirmed the encounter and stated that they had opened fire on the criminals only after giving them several warnings to surrender. Two policemen had received head injuries and bled profusely.

Incidentally, the same SP was also involved when three suspects involved in an acid attack were killed in an encounter. The victim of the acid attack had been raped and was going to court to stand witness when acid was thrown on her.

Congratulatory messages poured in, praising the police. Rose petals were showered on the police officials involved in the 'encounter'.

Social media went crazy at the outcome and the end that came for the heinous criminals. The entire nation, but for a handful of human rights activists, breathed a sigh of relief that justice had been served, that the Hyderabad Horror was finally over.